WORTH THE WAIT

A Book on Hope, Faith, Patience and Overcoming

Life's Hurdles

Published by

Right Side Publishing

P. O Box 339 Reynoldsburg, Ohio 43068

Print in the United States

Project manager Robert Cauley

Editor: M.O Blessing

Editor: Felicia S. Cauley

Editor: Monique Cooper

Cover design by

Interior Design by

ISBN-978-1-955050074

LCCN- 2022900850

This book may be purchased for educational, business, or sales promotional use. For information, kindly email the author
rightsideceo@yahoo.com
feliciacauley@ymail.com.
rightsideceo@yahoo.com
www.rightsidepiblishing.com

DEDICATION

This book is for all the young people going through the struggle of questioning their value and worth.

AKCNOWLEDGEMENT

I would like to thank the Lord, my savior Jesus Christ, my husband Robert who is my number one supporter, my children, Micleicia, John, Johnesha, Antalicia, my sister Kenyatta Alfred who is my right-hand person for reviewing my books, I love you dearly. To Shanna Pittman, who continues to challenge me to go above and beyond to explore different genre, to Monique Cooper, M. O Blessing, who helped bring my amazing vision to life on this book project. You both are heaven sent. And to all the readers of this wonderful piece, Remember Gods' way is the best way.

INTRODUCTION

Standing on the principles of God and doing the right things is not always easy. Angela with through compromising her standards only to find herself pregnant by a married man who was a drug dealer. She was (Tire of Waiting On God) the title of the first book. Read the first book you will learn her story. Angela was a young college graduate who got sick and tired of doing everything right and still ending up with the short end of the stick. Angela, who was raised by her mom Ashely and her Dad Spencer, spent most of her life with her Grandpa Miller and Grandmother Fannie Lee Peaches-Miller, where she was taught to love and obey God and his Word. Angela hung on to every teaching of her grandma.

And one can say that Grandma Peaches is the biggest influence on her life. She taught her mom Ashley the way of the Lord. Angela could not overcome her demons in the first book (Tire of Waiting on God.) She was hunted by life, captured, and sentenced into situations that could have claimed her freedom and leave her devastated for the rest of her life. However, despite being condemned and judged by friends and family after losing her baby and her childhood love she found out the hard way, God's way is the best way. Angela remained firm in her faith in God, and never ceased to talk to Him. Just as God says in his word in the book of Jeremiah 33:3, "Call unto me, and I will answer thee, and show thee great and mighty things, which thou knowest not." God in His precious mercy came through for Angela, hearkened unto her voice, wiped her tears, and set her back on her feet.

This time around, Angela was fortunate enough to pick up the pieces with the help of God. Worth The Wait is an interesting story that validates the statement, "The downfall of man is truly not the end of his life

TABLE OF CONTENTS

CHAPTER ONE

NEW BEGINNINGS.

Things changed in the blink of an eye, and Angela thanked God with a grateful heart. It seemed like yesterday her dating life was messy, and there was no light at the end of the tunnel. Moving and meeting Richard, her new boyfriend, opened new chapters in her life.

She was on cloud nine dating Richard, a godly man who had treated her well. He is tall, brown skin, he can sing, and play the guitar. Richard was clean cut, no sagging pants, or tattoos, body piercings, and wasn't pushing drugs in the hood, and has an exceptional work history, Richard comes from a God loving family, full of virtuous women, surrounded by the love of Christ, and he knows how to treat women.

There is a saying, "If a man treats his mother good, then he will treat his wife well". Angela took a sigh of relief and concentrated on her new career. Grandma Fannie Lee Peaches- Miller, fondly known as (Grandma Peaches) Papa Miller, Ashely, and Spencer, couldn't be happier for Angela.

"Now you got yourself a real man", Miss Fannie would tell her every time they talked on the phone.

It was the weekend, and Angela had nothing planned for the day, so she decided it would be a perfect day to relax and meditate on God. Angela was sitting on her bed as she contemplated what she could wear for the day. The sun was beaming outside her window, and she knew it was boiling hot outdoors, so she decided it might be best to wear a pair of shorts.

Angela wasn't the type of girl that would choose to wear something that was too revealing because of her religious beliefs as a Christian and therefore she selected shorts that were a decent length, almost reaching her knees. Angela made the perfect choice to keep her cool. She could be cute and modest. There was a time when she wouldn't dare wear shorts at all, although Angela had to admit that her Cousin Tina's sense of style and dress had influenced her own wardrobe choices.

Over a decent amount of time, Angela had realized that her relationship with God had developed her to maturity; therefore, she realized that if she dressed appropriately; she was certain of not overexposing herself, remaining modest and true to her beliefs.

Grandma Peaches and Papa Miller had raised her and her cousin Tina at the St Johns Baptist Church. Many of the members in that church community did not believe in wearing shorts at all, amongst many other things. For example, red lipstick wasn't the make-up to wear, and you shouldn't have your feet on display. If anyone wore earrings to service, they had to make sure they were modest. A clear lip-gloss would be more appropriate and long-sleeved garments... it isn't acceptable to have your arms showing. Grandma Peaches had always made sure that Angela and Tina adhered to the social rules and remained modest. However, as they had gotten older, everyone knew Tina did her own thing.

Angela was sitting in her room, preparing her clothes to relax around her apartment, when her phone suddenly rang. "Hello?" she answered.

"Hi, babe. How are you?" Richard asked. Angela smiled as she was happy to hear his pleasant voice over the phone.

"I'm doing great, Richard, just sitting here, picking out some clothes to wear today,"

"Where are you going, babe?" Richard asked curiously.

"Nowhere special. I have nothing planned. I just want to get dressed for the day. You know I always have to be dressed by noon, because I was raised that way by Grandma peaches, she would not have us lying around." Angela chuckled as she thought back on memories of Grandma Peaches having the girls dressed in the mornings.

"Well, since you have nothing to do, how about I pick you up and we can go get some lunch and hang out? I wanted to stop by the church for a little while to go over a song that just came to my mind. I'm thinking if it goes well, I might use it for the upcoming convention. What do you think?" Richard asked, sounding rather enthusiastic. Angela grinned as his enthusiasm was rubbing off on her.

"I would love to hear your new song," Angela responded proudly.

"Great, I'll pick you up about 11:30ish so we can have lunch first and then go by the church. Then afterwards we could take a walk together?"

Angela happily agrees and eventually ends the call with Richard to prepare for the new plans she has for the day.

Angela clicks her feet together; her heels touch each other as she could barely contain her excitement.

She had become so lost in thought about Richard that she had forgotten what she was doing prior to the phone call. She realized then that her shorts were still lying on the bed and remembered to choose an outfit for the day. She went through her closet, browsing the options, and pulled out a pink shirt. It was a lovely shirt, but perhaps a little too bright to wear for today. She put it back and instead picked out a blue blouse. It was beautiful; however, the arms were rather sheer. Then again, going out for lunch with Richard today was an important step in their relationship, as well as visiting the church together. Angela was sure that the church would be rather empty today and so the blue blouse would be fine to wear for herself and Richard's outing. She could still respect both her beliefs and look good for her boyfriend.

Angela took a quick shower and dressed before attempting to put on some light make-up. She used a clear colored mascara that was just enough to extend the length of her eyelashes and a bit of a natural blush on her face to accent her skin tone. She also uses a little eyeliner so they could barely see it but would bring out her eyes. Angela looked in the mirror once she had finished applying the blush to her face.

"Hmm, I don't know if I want to put on this lip gloss with the sparkles. I still want to distinguish myself and look like a Christian," Angela ponders out loud, looking at the lip-gloss in her hand.

However, there was a knock at the door and Angela thought it was Richard. Angela opened the bathroom door to peek her head out just to make sure that it was a knock. There was a second knock and

Angela realized she had better hurry and finish her makeup before heading towards the front door of her apartment.

"Just a minute, I hear you, I'm coming right now", Angela says racing towards the door. She opens the door with a grin, which morphs into a surprised expression as she notices it wasn't Richard at the door, but in fact, her cousin Tina.

"What are you doing here?" Angela asked.

"Well, nice to see you too, cuz", Tina replied with a little sarcastic tone, however she still maintained a bright smile.

"I'm sorry, I thought you were Richard because he's picking me up for lunch," Angela explained.

"I thought I talked to you last week, and you told me you didn't have to work this weekend? I figured you wouldn't have anything to do, so I thought we could hang out", Tina responded. She maintained her smile; however, Angela could notice her sadness and disappointment. She didn't want to turn Tina away and therefore thought of a plan that could keep them both happy. After all, she had traveled all the way from Alabama to visit her.

"Since you're no stranger, I hate to do this to you, but I have plans with Richard, so how about you stay here and hangout in my apartment until we get back, we won't be long, I promise?", Angela asked. Tina sighed and shrugged her shoulders.

"You know what Angela; I've changed a lot, so I will not complain. You know, back in the day; I probably would have been a little jealous and demand that since I'm your first cousin, I should probably come first before any man. Things are different now. I have a couple of friends here, so I suppose I could call and meet up with them. I don't think I'll surprise them. That doesn't seem to be such a good idea," Tina sighed.

Angela nodded her head, with agreement. She was happy that Tina had somewhere to go and that her trip wouldn't go to waste.

"When you get back later, let me know when you're free. I'm going to stick around for the next couple of days. I might even extend my time here for a week. I haven't decided yet," Tina said thoughtfully.

"I really hope you choose to stay a week longer. I really want to hang out with you. I'm off work next weekend and have a few days off on weekdays. Perhaps I could adjust my schedule depending on yours. It's the least I could do considering you came all this way out to visit me," Angela smiled, hoping to make it up to Tina.

"Okay cousin, I'll see you later. I'd better leave before Richard gets here, don't worry, I don't want to intrude and hold you guys up because I love to talk to Richard. I must admit that he is a joy to be around and brilliant. I'm thrilled the two of you are together. You must be proud, Angela," Tina smiles.

Angela chuckles and then gives Tina a hug. They wrap their arms around one another and squeeze themselves into a tight and warm embrace. "You better not leave without getting in touch with me, so the two of us can plan to hang out", Angela said, separating them both from the hug.

Tina chuckles and then moves to open the door for herself. She slowly turned back to look at Angela.

"I promise I won't. Now have fun and do nothing I wouldn't do. Then again, I know the two of you will always be godly and respectable. Bye girl", Tina said before finally leaving and closing the door behind herself.

Fifteen minutes had passed by before there was another knock on her door. Angela was confident that it was Richard this time, and though she swung her front door open to find him standing in the doorway, he was holding a beautiful bouquet in his hands. "Richard, I didn't know you wanted to stop by your mother's house, I wish you told be you were going to bring her flowers, I would have brought something myself", Angela asked, looking a little disheartened that she didn't have the chance to bring his mother something nice from herself.

Richard put his head down in disbelief and chuckled, "Angela, you are something else. My mother was sick with the flu over a week ago. I'm happy you're still thinking of her, but my mother is better. I brought these flowers for you," He said handing, the flowers to her. Angela accepted them with a bright smile on her face

"Thank you, Richard. I'm sorry I didn't realize. Your mother had been on my mind for a while. I knew she was sick and didn't realize how long ago it was. Either way, I'm grateful she has recovered and is feeling better," Angela responded with a warm smile, running her fingertips gently along the flower petals before finding a vase with water to place her flowers in.

"That is why I love you so much, because you have a big and caring heart", Richard said, grabbing Angela and pulling her into a hug. Angela chuckled, and Richard begun to playfully squeeze and tickle her.

"Richard, we're going to be late for lunch", Angela said through her laughter. Richard laughed and then held onto Angela's hand, lacing their fingers together. He guided her out of her apartment and out to the porch towards where he had parked. When Angela lifted her head, she noticed the beautiful red convertible car that was parked on the road with its roof down. Angela instantly turned to stare at Richard with shock and excitement.

"Wow, Richard, look at this, I love your car", Angela exclaimed as they approached his car and she circled around it in awe. She kept repeating about how much she loved it and its tan hardtop paint.

"Thank you, babe, you know have your license and this is actually my second car, it's best I use it on special occasions, but I will let you drive it if you need to," Richard offered, smiling as he watched Angela circle his car with a bright smile on her face.

"Thank you, Richard, I have my car and I don't want to get used to driving something like this", Angela responded. She would love to take it for a spin, but it was expensive, and she didn't want to ruin his care that he took care of.

"Angela, did you hear what I said? This car is for special occasions. I really don't even drive it all the time, but I mean, if you and Tina or perhaps your other friends want to hang out together, I'd class that as a special occasion."

"Wow, Richard, you are the best. We aren't even married yet and you're already giving me permission to drive your sports car," Angela said with a cheeky grin.

"Don't speak too soon because that might happen eventually", Richard said, approaching Angela and holding gently onto her shoulder. He almost laughed at the bright pink blush that adorned her features as she avoided eye contact.

"You know Angela, we've been dating for a while. Almost six months and still counting. You know at our church they say that if you have been dating for six months, you should know by then if it is the person you wish to marry or not... I'm just saying," he said, his hands still gently holding onto Angela.

"I agree with you, Richard, and I'm not scared of being with you. I have already envisioned my life with you. It's just... weddings are very expensive, and I know there's so much that I want, so I wanted us to take time out. I know everything about you and my family approve of you. I promise that romantically we're on the same page, financially it's different," Angela said, placing her own hands on his shoulder to reassure him of her feelings.

Richard grinned from ear-to-ear.

"Well, that's a relief!" Richard laughed and laughed.

CHAPTER TWO

BUILDING NEW RELATIONSHIPS

It was a warm evening and Angela had spent most of her evening alone. It was one of the rare days she had got off work. Tina had declared herself busy for the day. Therefore, Angela had picked a book from her bookshelf and curled up on her sofa. She chose a non-fictional book on improving mindfulness and drank a warm cup of coffee she had made for herself whilst relaxing. Suddenly, the phone rang, and she saw it was Richard.

Angela was settling down in Atlanta. She had not seen Richard since their last lunch date. He was busy composing music for the church. Angela love to date men who loved God and music. What a combination!

"Hello Richard", She answered enthusiastically. She was always happy to hear his voice after a long day of being on her own.

"Hello my love, how have you been this evening?" He asked.

Angela chuckled with glee at his statement. It never failed to warm her up whenever Richard would refer to her so lovingly. It was a nice and wonderful feeling to feel so treasured by someone else. She smiled and placed her book on the counter side. "I've been happy and spending some time on self-reflection, though I must admit I have missed your presence", she admitted.

Richard chuckled at her response, "Well, if you aren't too busy, I was hoping I could take you out for dinner tonight?"

Angela perked up in her seat with excitement. "I'm always happy to go on a date with you", she said truthfully, thinking back on all the earlier occasions in which Richard would come by and sweep her off her feet.

"That's perfect! I can come and pick you up around 6pm, if that's alright with you?" Richard asked. Angela looked up towards the clock that hung in her living room and noticed that it was already 5pm. She would have an hour to pick out the perfect outfit and makeup.

"Yes, yes, that's perfect. I can't wait to see you!"

"Nor can I. I love you and I'll see you later," Richard responded.

"I love you too, goodbye", Angela exclaimed before hanging up the phone. She jumped to her feet excitedly and ran as quickly as she could towards her bedroom. She rummaged through her wardrobe looking for something acceptable, modest, and elegant to wear. Angela wanted Richard to see how beautiful and respectful she could look. Eventually, she wore a white blouse, with a lengthy, flowing skirt that was the appropriate length. She applied light makeup, following a few tips she had learned from Tina. Before finishing her look by wearing her small necklace with a cross around her neck.

Once she had finished dressing, an hour had already passed, and she received a text from Richard informing her he was outside waiting for her.

"You look beautiful", Richard said, once Angela had left her apartment and had walked over to meet Richard at his car. He leaned down to place a soft kiss on her cheek before opening the car door like a gentleman and allowing her to take a seat. Gospel FM had been playing music on the radio and he rolled down his car windows as the warm evening wind ran through Angela's hair during the drive. Tonight, was the perfect night for a date.

"So, are you going to tell me where we are going?" Angela asked curiously, looking over towards Richard who smirked, although his eyes never left the road.

"I thought you would like a surprise,"

"I'd like anything you give me", Angela whispered under her breath. She turned to look back outside of her window and enjoy the sights of the world passing them by. The sun wasn't due to set for another couple hours, however Angela thought perhaps it might be romantic to watch the sunset with Richard towards the end of their date. Before they knew it, Angela realized Richard was pulling into the posh and high-end area of the town.

She was even more surprised to find that Richard was taking her towards the new and prestigious restaurant in town.

"The Clio Lounge?", She asked, looking up at the restaurant sign.

"A beautiful, respectable establishment. I think you're worth only the best. I think your father would approve of such a place," Richard grinned, feeling rather proud that he could impress Angela and show her the finer things in life.

"Let us not wait outside, only longer", He said with a grin and took a hold of Angela's hand. He walked up to the door and held the door open for her. They were both escorted to a table at the back of the restaurant. Angela looked in awe of the establishment. It was bright and beautiful inside. It had a very rustic and authentic aesthetic that Angela favored.

"Drinks?", The server asked them both.

"I think we both would like a tonic water and lime?", Richard ordered for them both. He remembered what Angela had always liked to drink.

"You look stunned", Richard commented, reaching out across the table to take her hand in his.

"I am. I appreciate how lovely it looks here. It makes me happy that you thought of this place for us," Angela said with a shy smile.

"You never leave my mind, Angela."

Both Angela and Richard had a wonderful evening together. The food had been excellent. Angela had really enjoyed the lasagna dish that she had ordered, whereas Richard had gone for a salmon dish that looked just as appetizing. They talked a lot whilst they ate. Richard spoke a lot about how his studies within in the church were going, along with his application process to be an ordained pastor. Angela was excited for him. The two of them had been finishing up their meals when Richard had noticed a couple of friends from the church that were nearby. It was Angela who insisted that he invite them over.

"Sister Elaine, Sister Martha, it's a pleasure to see you both out tonight. You know Angela, of course," Richard said as the two older women had approached the couple.

Sister Elaine chuckled and tapped Richard playfully on the shoulder.

"We told you Richard, just Elaine and Martha will do. As for this lovely young woman, we're very pleased to see you again," Elaine said, turning towards Angela with a wise smile while lightly hugging her in greeting her.

"It was at the last service we spoke to one another, was it not?" Martha had asked.

"Yes, it was. I was happy meeting you. Please sit for a while", Angela grinned and showed the space next to herself and then the space next to Richard.

"Oh, we wouldn't want to intrude on your evening."

"We don't mind, it's great for me to meet new people from the church. It has only been six months",

Angela insisted with love, allowing Elaine to sit next to her, while Martha had sat down next to Richard.

"Yes, it has. It can be hard moving away from home, but building relationships in our community can help with the loneliness," Martha said, sounding very similar to Grandma Peaches and her initial concern for Angela moving away from home.

"I've never been happier", Angela said, smiling over at Richard.

The four of them could converse easily with one another. Angela knew she had seen the women before, but she didn't know them every well. She was very pleased to find out that they were a part of the choir and were thrilled to perform the new songs that Richard would bring to service. Elaine and Martha had been extremely kind and welcoming to Angela and had invited her to attend the bible study sessions they would lead every fortnight. Angela had happily agreed. They also listened to Angela talk about her Grandma Peaches and wished to exchange recipes with her.

Eventually, the two women bid the couple goodbye and Angela and Richard could end their date on a hopeful and positive note, Angela had also made sure that the two of them could watch the sunset before Richard decided it was time to get Angela back home.

Richard turned towards Angela on the drive back home. "Did you have a nice evening?"

"It was amazing, I'm so happy that I got to spend time with you, and I really enjoyed having a thorough conversation with the ladies from the church,

I think it's always good for me to go out there and build new relationships," Angela responded.

"They have been a solid part of the community for years. I'm glad you had the chance to bond with them. It's important to me you are happy here," Richard said sincerely.

"I'm happy too,"

Angela and Richard smiled at one another and were once again grateful for another blessed day.

CHAPTER THREE

THE SWINGERS

I t was a Sunday afternoon and the members of the church had slowly trickled out of the church at the end of service. Usually, people would chat for a little while before going straight home. However, a few members had congregated in front of the church as a few sisters were selling cakes and flapjacks they had made for contributions to go towards the church. Richard and Angela had stayed behind together and conversed with a few members, especially those who wished to talk to Richard and ask how his journey to becoming an ordained pastor was going.

"It was great to see you again, Angela. We will see you next week?" Martha asked as she walked by with a smile. Since bumping into Martha and Elaine earlier that week, the two women had taken Angela under her wing and had sat with her during the service today.

"Yes, I will see you next week", Angela said happily, waving the woman goodbye.

"Perfect, I'll be going now and get home safely," Martha smiled and waved in return.

Angela hung around for a while as she silently waited for Richard to wrap up his conversation. The two of them had agreed to go grocery shopping together after the service had finished. Angela wanted to make a pleasant home cooked meal for Richard and insisted that he come and help her choose something that he would enjoy. However, she would not rush his conversation with their church's current pastor. It was most likely about something important.

It was then that her phone rang, and she saw it was Grandma Peaches. Angela grinned as she answered the phone. It had been a while since she and her grandmother had last caught up with one another.

"Hello Grandma Peaches", Angela said happily.

"Hello Angela, it's been a moment since I've heard your darling voice. Have you finished service already?", Grandma Peaches asked in that soft, loving tone that she had always talked in. Angela felt as though listening to Grandma Peaches talk was like a breath of fresh air, but it also made her miss home and her family just a little more than she already did. She made a mental note to visit home sometime soon.

"Yes, we left the church just a moment ago. Is Ashley with you?" Angela inquired.

"She was just a moment ago, you know how she is full of life, here one moment busy doing something else the next", Grandma Peaches said with a hearty laugh which Angela couldn't help but return. She always loved the way Grandma Peaches laughed and was grateful that it would never change.

"I was just calling to see how you are doing. Have you made any new friends? Is Richard treating you well?", She asked. Angela could tell, despite her curiosity, that Grandma Peaches was still feeling very concerned about Angela's well-being and how she was coping away from home. She only wished that Richard really was doing a good job looking after her and helping her create lasting relationships.

"Yes, Grandma Peaches. Richard is treating me very well. I have made a couple of church friends; I think you would like them. In fact, did you get the recipe I texted you the other day?" Angela asked.

Grandma Peaches exclaimed gleefully, as she remembered the message she had received from Angela, "Yes I did, I made a lovely sweet potato pie yesterday, I'll have to send you a picture of it", she giggled. Angela missed the way Grandma Peaches used to cook. There wasn't anything as spectacular as her food and suddenly she felt a little homesick and was missing her childhood meals.

Grandma Peaches carried on talking in Angela's ear about what had been happening at home and what changes they had made in her absence; however, Angela's attention had been drawn to what appeared to be a couple who were loitering around near the church. They were not people that had attended the church before. Angela knew almost all their members. However, something about them appeared as though they wanted someone to talk to.

"Grandma Peaches, I'm going to have to go, but I will call you later with more news", Angela stated, slowly making her way over to the couple who stood outside their car.

"Of course, dear, I'll hear from you later."

Once Grandma Peaches hung up the phone, Angela looked back towards Richard and found that he was still in conversation. Therefore, she took a deep breath and walked over towards the couple, who noticed her approaching. They looked like a normal and happy couple; they were dressed in a way that perhaps wasn't appropriate for a service, but Angela would not judge someone for what they wore. They appeared very curious as Angela stood in front of them with a wide smile.

"It's a beautiful day today", she stated, looking up towards the bright sun that gleamed above their heads.

They both smiled and nodded their heads. Angela noticed that the woman kept glancing at the church behind her.

"We just finished our service today, but if you would like one of these, it's everything the church offers during the week, as well as our regular Sunday service", Angela said, handing out a couple brochures that she always carried around with her. They both happily took one and looked over it. After a moment, the woman looked up with a careful smile and glanced again towards the church.

"Your church... is it accepting?" She asked carefully.

"We accept people from all walks of life. It is not for us to judge for him", Angela replied, glancing up happily towards the heavens. The woman smiled at Angela's sincerity, however she still appeared to be uncertain.

"I'm afraid mine and my husband's way of life may interfere with the agenda of your church,"

Angela tilted her head to the side in confusion. She wasn't certain what the women was referring to and didn't want to push for an answer, in case the couple didn't want to elaborate. The woman sighed and then leaned forward to whisper to Angela, making sure that nobody could overhear her.

"We're swingers,"

Angela was rather shocked. She knew what swingers were and the lifestyle they lived. Angela was adamantly opposed to having a relationship like theirs and her Grandma Peaches would be most horrified. Then again, Angela learned that it still wasn't her place to judge people on the less than better decisions they may make in their life. There must be a reason such a couple had come today and were inquiring about her church.

"I see", Angela said, attempting to conceal her shock.

"It was fun for us. It was a way for us to connect more during our marriage. We haven't been married too long, and we were uncertain how to maintain the love between us, so adding another couple to the equation worked for us," the woman said with an uneasy smile.

"This is something you wish to do for a long time?" Angela asked.

The couple shared a quick glance with one another, before they both shook their heads, "It's something we have already done for a long time, we're just not sure it's something we can continue to do", The woman's husband had said, speaking up for the first time. The husband tells her that his wife is not fulfilling the needs that he has for him to be satisfied in their bedroom and that he needs something more than what she can give him and that he needs to have sex with other women The couple sees them as friends, and when they talk to them, they try to set them up with other couples they know. They talk of the word of God, but they do not know God. They come to church and do their thing. They are pretending to be what they are not. They are not leading by example. Nowadays; people have lost the true meaning of being a Christian. It is all about going to church, singing, and praying. They have not learned to live a life that is of God's will. They are living a double life. They are living a life that is inconsistent with the word of God. Many people nowadays claim to be Christians, yet their actions do not reflect this. They do not live according to God's word. They attend church and carry on with their daily lives. They sing and pray, but they are unaware of God's existence. They haven't changed. They've never heard of God before. They do not live according to God's word. Other's Faith is put to the test regularly, but they weather the storms of life. The ones who do not live according to God's word. They do not follow

God's commandments. They put on a show, but it doesn't change the fact that they are who they are. Their actions are contradictory to their professed faith. Many people believe in God but do not live by his word. They do not lead a life that is consistent with His holy word. They do not do what the word says they should do. People often get involved with the church because they want to be ministered to. They want to hear a wonderful sermon. They want someone to talk to them about God. Suppose a person is not living a life that is consistent with the word of God. They are not living as a Christian should. They are not living a life that is consistent with the word of God! They do not do what the word says to do. Many people claim to be Christians but do not carry out their faith. We are not the only ones living this type of lifestyle, Angela! The husband replied sternly.

Angela thought for a moment about what the couple had said. It was clear that the couple had lived and acted promiscuously for a while. Not every couple within the church has lived a happy and perfect life with their spouse. However, this is the first time Angela had met such a couple. Although Angela understood the man and woman before her may seek a higher purpose and were hoping to turn away from swinging and find a healthier, happier, and more spiritual way to maintain their marriage, before the eyes of God.

"You know, the bible can teach us a lot of oneself and our relationships. I know that both myself and Richard connect through these teachings. Perhaps this is something that you could learn?" Angela said, pointing towards the pamphlet that the woman was holding in her hand.

"You really think so?" she asked, appearing hopeful.

Angela nodded with a bright smile, "It's a healthier and happier lifestyle. I think you may enjoy his teachings and can yet find a path to follow... come to service and see for yourself."

The couple had agreed to try out their next service and had introduced themselves as Holly and Cameron. They smiled kindly at Angela before getting in their car and driving away. Angela had to admit that she was still curious about the lifestyle they had previously chosen to live. However, Angela knew that sometimes people hear their calling to God and to the church at different times in their lives.

Angela felt an arm wrap around her shoulder as Richard had finally finished his conversation and was walking her towards his car.

"Who were they?", Richard asked, nodding his head in the direction that the couple of drove away in.

"A married couple, I think they may be curious about what the church could offer,"

"Is that all?", He asked.

Angela debated about whether to share with Richard what she knew about their lifestyle. In the end, she decided not to. She concluded it was neither their place to judge what they had done in their life if they were here now and were deciding to follow a happier path.

"Just people wishing to better themselves..."

CHAPTER FOUR

THE ENGAGEMENT.

It was on a cold evening that Angela had received a text message from Richard, asking if she could meet him just after sunset at the Market Place in town. The nighttime markets were popular for being a very romantic spot, where couples can buy little trinkets together or have a warm cup of hot cocoa with one another. They were very similar to the markets that the town put on during Christmas time. Angela also knew the downtown markets also had an outdoor ice-skating rink. Perhaps this was the date idea that Richard had in mind.

Angela was standing in her room, once again contemplating what would be perfect to wear for the night, when there was a sudden knock on her living room door. She knew that it most likely wasn't Richard and therefore wasn't too shocked to find Tina on the other side of the door.

"Tina? What are you doing here?" Angela asked, not expecting her cousin again.

"I'm here to see you, of course", I only live about three hours away from you. Have you forgotten Atlanta is less than three hours from Alabama? Tina said with a wide grin before inviting herself inside of Angela's apartment and plopping onto her couch. Angela was always happy to see Tina. However, she felt very guilty about the bad timing that had happened once again. It was probably best that Tina informed her when she was going to drop by in the future.

"Tina, I'm so sorry to do this to you again, but I'm going out with Richard tonight. He wants me to meet him in the town markets," Angela said with a very guilty smile.

"Girl relax, why do you think I'm here? He asked me to make sure you aren't panicking over what to wear and to drive you downtown," Tina said, twirling her car keys in her hand.

Angela squealed aloud with excitement and raced over to where Tina was sitting before grabbing her by her wrist and dragging her into her bedroom. She was happy that she could have this small amount of time to hang out with her cousin, but also have her help with choosing something to wear. The two of them settled on a beautiful black dress that hit just a little before her knees. Tina had also escorted Angela over to a chair by her vanity mirror and prepared to do her hair and makeup for her.

"Remember, I like my makeup rather subtle", Angela reminded her, as she remembered that Tina sometimes had the tendency to go a little overboard with applying color to her eyelids.

"Relax cousin, I promise I won't go overboard," Tina reassured her.

The two of them have a lovely and quiet time together. They talk little as Angela focused too much on keeping still so Tina wouldn't get distracted and smudge the makeup look she was doing for her. Once Tina had finished Angela's makeup, she helped her cousin to her feet and chuckled when Angela gave Tina a twirl.

"Do you think this is too much? I don't think we're going for something to eat. Maybe I should get changed", Angela said, suddenly doubting the way she looked. She tried to rush and walk past Tina to get changed into something else, however Tina grabbed her by the arm and pulled her back in front of the mirror and was shaking her head at her.

"I don't think so Angela, you look beautiful, and I wouldn't worry about being overdressed. I might have a little clue about what Richard wants to do tonight, and I promise you are dressed appropriately," Tina said with a little smug smile.

Angela was becoming even more impatient and excited by tonight's prospects. She really wanted to know what exactly Richard had in store for her. However, she didn't want to ruin the element of surprise and avoided begging Tina for an answer. Tina was driving Angela through the town and towards the markets. The cousins had a moment to talk and laugh with one another before Tina was pulling into a parking spot to drop her off.

"Wait, where do I go?" Angela asked, feeling rather lost and looking at the entrance of the markets.

"Richard told me to tell you to follow the white roses,"

Angela was confused and wasn't sure about what Tina had meant. That was until a worker who was in a market stall nearby walked towards Angela with a bright smile on their face and handed her a white rose, before pointing her in the direction they expected her to go. Angela could hear Tina laughing at her shock and waved her goodbye, before turning back around to collect some more white roses.

Something about this felt very romantic and lighthearted as she followed the path and gifts of the white roses. Before she knew it, there was a bunch of roses that had gathered in her hands, and it had led her to the ice-skating rink downtown in Atlanta.

The person who was working on the ice-skating rink noticed Angela almost immediately and had carefully taken the loose bunch of flowers in her hand and wrapped them together in a beautiful, white silk bow. The worker reached out and gave Angela a pair of ice-skates.

"Put these on and meet your date out in the ice,"

Angela smiled warmly and put on her ice-skate before skating out onto the ice with the floral bouquet in her hands. Suddenly, Richard had skated on the ice, appearing from nowhere with a huge, cheesy grin on his face. He reached down to hold her free hand and the pair of them skated together.

"Do you like your roses?"

"They're absolutely beautiful, thank you. This is our most elaborate date yet Richard, I can't believe you have thought all of this through," Angela praised him.

"Well, this isn't all. I think there's some people over there to see you."

Richard pointed out to a group of people that were standing by the side of the skating rink. She didn't know who it could have been at first, but as she skated closer, she realized it was Tina, Ashley, Spencer, grandma Peaches, Grandpa Miller, Michelle, and her husband all stood by the side, watching her with matched grins. Angela squealed with excitement and euphoria as she quickly skated over to her group of friends and family and pulled Grandma Peaches into a huge, tight hug.

"Wow! I can't believe you're all here! Nobody told me you were all coming down", Angela yelled with barely concealed excitement. She tried her hardest to hold happy tears in her eyes.

"Well, of course not dear, or else it wouldn't be a surprise,"

"I'm absolutely over the moon that you are all here, but why are you all here right now", Angela asked, stepping back to look at the rather mischievous faces of the people she loved.

"We couldn't miss this special occasion," Spencer finally said

"What special occasion?", Angela asked, maintaining her smile. Her family and friends didn't answer her, however they looked behind Angela with the widest grins she had seen anyone have all year. Angela slowly turned around to see what they were looking at and instantly felt overwhelmed with shock and elation when she saw they were looking at Richard, who was on one knee and holding up a ring in a velvet box.

"My beautiful Angela. I know you're rather shocked right now. But I couldn't imagine doing this without the people you care about being here as our witnesses. We have been dating long enough for me to realize that you are the person who I want to live the rest of my life with. You are caring, loving, and have such an enormous heart. I only wish that your heart is wide enough to accept me as your forever loving husband, so Angela, I must ask, will you do me the honor of becoming my wife?"

Angela was in complete shock and couldn't stop the tears that were flowing down her face. She knew what they had talked about before and wanted nothing more than to live her life with Richard. She just didn't expect that he would love her so much that he wanted to marry her too soon. Her heart was so full and content and she didn't know what to say, so she stuttered.

"I think what she's trying to say is yes, absolutely," Tina teased, and Spencer nudged her playfully.

Angela finally laughed out loud at Tina's comment and realized that everything she ever wanted was right before her. She loved Richard; he was the perfect man for her, and she thought that there was no one better for her.

"Yes! Yes, I will marry you,"

Angela was happy to declare her love for Richard before her family and, most of all, before God.

Chapter Five:

Richard is ordained as Pastor.

Angela was in the church during the regular Sunday service. This was her first-time seeing people since Richard had finally popped the question earlier that week and, as she expected, many members of the church who had heard the news wanted to know the full story about how Richard had proposed. Angela looked around and found the swinging couple. Holly and Cameron had attended church, after all. Angela hoped they wouldn't continue their double lives and continued down the path of Christianity.

Angela was sitting at the front in between both Martha and Elaine, who couldn't help but gossip almost the entire way through the surface. Martha reached out and held Angela's hand as she inspected the beautiful diamond ring on her finger with a jolly expression.

"Look at that beautiful piece of jewelry. I wish my husband had gotten me something as wonderful as that," Martha teased, showing off her very own old-fashioned wedding ring.

"That isn't everything, though. I hear the way Richard proposed was spectacular. Please share the story with us, Angela," Elaine pleaded, holding onto the other side of Angela.

Angela couldn't help but giggle aloud at their antics and eventually gave in and told them her engagement story. It was nice to share these sorts of things with the new friends that she had made, "It was so beautiful, he had me follow a trail of white roses, it was as though I was already a bride and then I found all my family from home were there so I had gotten a little suspicious, then I realized he had invited them out to witness us getting engaged, he's made me happier than I could even imagined", Angela said, smiling brightly at the ring on her finger and she realized she was going to be somebodies wife reasonably soon.

Both Martha and Elaine had cooed and swooned at Angela's story.

"I love a good proposal. Are the two of you looking to tie the knot soon?" Elaine asked.

"Not yet, I've always dreamed of a huge wedding, so I know we need to take our time with saving and making sure we can afford it first", Angela stated. She was grateful that both she and Richard had discussed their financial situation before he had proposed, therefore there was no rush for the two of them to be married but allowed the both to focus on making sure they could afford the luxurious wedding the two of them deserved.

Finally, the ordination ceremony was beginning. Richard's ordination application had finally been approved, and he had passed the studies he had been doing through the church. Today was the day that Richard would finally become an ordained pastor. The service started off with two hymns for the church to sing together. The hymns were a formal part of the ceremony.

Richard delivers his own scripture during the service and then the traditional roles and parts of the ceremony took place. Angela felt so proud and happy to witness Richard on his special day and felt blessed about how much closer they were getting to God. Eventually, Richard was presented with a special bible that commemorates his fully ordained ministry status. They concluded the service with a benediction.

At the end, everyone in the church had applauded because they were proud of what Richard had achieved. Richard smiled graciously and bowed his head. The current pastor of the church offered a wide grin and offered Richard a firm handshake.

"Welcome Pastor Richard and it is also our pleasure to announce the engagement of Pastor Richard and his Fiancée Angela to the church, may we pray, give them our blessings and congratulations", Everyone clapped again and this time some of the church had turned towards Angela and congratulated her. Angela felt very shy to have everyone's eyes on her, however she smiled and accepted her well wishes, regardless.

"I will now lead the choir with a song", Richard said and turned towards the churches choir. The whole church was up on their feet, dancing and singing with the choir's song. Angela looked around at the church and took in the elation on the members' faces. She turned then to look back at her fiancé and was astonished by how he led people with ease. It was then that Angela really felt like she was in a place that she truly belonged to and felt blessed once again that this was her life.

After the service. A few members of the church had congregated outside in the church courtyard and had instantly sought both Richard and Angela to offer their congratulations on their engagement. They gazed at the ring that Richard had chosen for her with sparkles in their eyes. Another member of the church had then asked Richard if he would do what he intended to do? Now that he was a pastor, he could ordain pastors at his own church.

"I haven't gotten an exact plan; however, I have been emailed earlier that week with the opportunity to lead a choir song within the Mega church", Richard said proudly. Angela turned to look at him with wide-eyed, that was the first time she had heard anything about Richard performing or speaking within a Mega-church, that was a huge deal for him and if all were to go well, it might be the start of something big for them both.

"The Mega-church? That's an amazing opportunity. Can you believe that you're already moving onto amazing and great things? You must be very proud of your fiancé," the member asked, turning to look towards Angela, who was still staring at Richard with awe.

"I'm very proud of him,"

Everyone wished everyone a good afternoon, and Richard was free to escort Angela to his car and drive her home. Once he had stopped at a red light, he took a moment to look at the ring on her finger and realized he was so happy just to see it there "Everybody is right you know, this ring looks especially beautiful on your finger", He said.

"It's beautiful because you put it there," Angela grinned with excitement.

Richard smiled at her and then laid a gentle kiss on her hands.

"So, what do you think about going with me next week?" He asked.

"To the Mega Church?", She questioned. Angela was still feeling rather unsure about attending a mega-church. She felt as though she had only just met all the members of their current church and there was a vast, staggering number of people who would attend a mega-church. It would be quite difficult to form a relationship with any of them.

"I'm happy to follow you anywhere. I'm just not ready to leave this church behind. I hope we can stay and worship here," she asked.

"Of course, I don't intend to leave this choir completely, and the service I do is a big chance for me and a huge step for my first message as an ordained pastor, I only wish for you to be there when I lay the foundations,"

"I wouldn't miss it for the world", Angela said, and she meant it.

CHAPTER SIX:

THE MEGA-CHURCH

Today was the first day that Angela and Richard would attend the Mega church, Solid Rock Christian Faith, known as SRCF. Angela could already tell that she would miss the regular service at their own church. However, she was really looking forward to how different of an experience this was going to be. Today was going to be a big step for Richard. It was going to be his first time reading to an audience as an ordained pastor and leading an important choir procession in front of thousands of worshippers. Angela thought that with a bit of hard work and support, Richard may have the chance of running his own Mega church one day and Angela could be more actively involved in the community.

Angela couldn't wait to call home and tell Grandma Peaches all about what their day had in store. She also had told Michelle and her husband. Whose name is Charles. Angela just refers to him as Michelle's husband. It is still hard for her to say the name Charles. It reminds her too much of her Charles from her past. Although Michelle's husband is far from a drug dealer. Michelle would have probably attended the service with her if it wasn't for them being so incredibly occupied. None the less, Angela still had her cousin Tina, who jumped at the chance to come to the service with them and support Richard.

"Are you sure I'm going to be good company for you today?" Tina asked consciously.

"Of course, you are. This is an important day for us both. Who knows what may happen today? I hear

this church usually has a lot of celebrity performers",
Angela said with excitement. She had been up the
night before and had been watching videos of previous
mega church services on YouTube. It looked to be both
intimidating and powerful, having so many followers
in one room, feeling the music of the gospel and
relating to the scriptures and teachings.

"So that's the dream, is it? Tina asked, pulling
Angela out of her daydream.

"What?", Angela asked.

"To one day run a mega-church of your own. I
bet Richard would be great enough to take over one
almost right away. It won't be long until you will run
something yourself within his church," Tina assumed.

Angela shrugged. She had thought little about
what she would do for sure when Richard had the

chance to run and ordain his own church or services. There might have been a little something that she could help and contribute towards.

"What would you like to do for the church?" Tina asked, wanting an answer. She could see the cogwheels turning in Angela's head as she thought hard and thoroughly about what she really might want to do.

"I'm unsure. I think I would like to be a lot like Grandma Peaches. She was strict, but she also helped a lot of the youth when we were young and growing up in the church, I thought perhaps that I had a similar calling and could also have Richard help me with helping the youth within, and outside of the church," Angela concluded. It didn't sound like much of a plan when spoken out loud, but it was a definite idea that could be further built upon and completed when given the proper time and planning.

Tina nodded her head in approval.

"You really have turned out to be a fine young woman, cousin, and Wow, you are 25 years old, and engaged! Both you and your fiancé are saints," Tina said, playfully bumping Angela on the shoulder.

They share a chuckle, before Angela looked over to the clock and realized that the time had flown by, "My goodness, look at the time! We better start heading over to service", she said, jumping out of her seat and texting Richard, wondering how far he was away from the apartment.

Eventually, Richard pulls up in his car and drives the three of them towards the service. When they pulled up in the parking lot, they noticed that the mega-church was enormous compared to the size of an ordinary church. It was a vast arena that was already full to the brim with guests. They considered Richard to be a special guest and therefore the three of them had seats reserved right at the front of the stage. Angela looked around to see cameras all around the arena. She assumed that this was because the service was being livestreamed to the thousands of Christian worshippers who were watching from home.

When the service started, Angela understood why mega churches were so popular. There was something intense and beautiful about having all these people praising God in one room. The pastor was enthusiastic and attention grabbing; he knew how to lead a room. Richard would learn a lot from watching these kinds of services. After a while, the pastor called Richard forward to join him on stage. Angela was exceptionally proud and emotional to see her fiancé up there.

Richard introduced himself to the church and read out a scripture for the worshippers before explaining all that he was grateful for and then leading his first song with the church's choir, there were famous singers in the audience who were singing and nodded approvingly at Richards' direction.

"He's a natural, isn't he?" Tina asked, leading in towards Angela.

"Yes, he is", Angela said and despite the little bundle of nerved she felt in her stomach for Richard, she was in awe of him and his ability to command a choir. It was as though he did everything in God's careful direction.

Angela couldn't believe that this man was going to be her husband.

The service continued for another couple of hours. Richard was only meant to lead a couple of songs during the service, but his character and his teachings were favored by the Mega-church's pastor, and he was therefore invited to stay on the stage longer for the two of them to preach together. For a moment, Angela allowed herself to think of what it may really be like to lead a mega-church of her own. Her future husband would ordain the services, of course, but there were so many things that Angela could run, such as a Sunday school, or youth services that would help the youth of today.

They were almost there.

At the end of the service, Richard, Angela, and Tina had stayed behind to converse with the leaders of the mega-church, including the pastor who had invited Richard to stay on stage with him for much longer than planned.

"You must be the wonderful Angela, Richard has spoken about you", The pastor said as Angela and Tina approached where the two men had been quietly conversing with one another. Angela chuckled and pleasantly shook his hand.

"Yes sir, that would be me,"

"Is that an engagement ring? I see, I suppose congratulations are in order. Planning on getting married anytime soon? "The pastor asked kindly, looking at Richard and Angela. Richard chuckled and held Angela's hand in his own.

"Thank you, pastor, we're not in any rush to tie the knot. We want to make sure we are settled and in a stable financial place before burning the money in our bank accounts. We're focusing more on our work within the church. I hadn't mentioned it before, but I know Angela had a few ideas about youth programs that could be put in place. It's all about keeping vulnerable children off the streets and opening their eyes to a loving, Christian community," Richard.

said, lovingly squeezing Angela's hand.

Angela quickly gazed down at her feet in embarrassment. However, the pastor was looking at her as though what he had heard was the best thing he had heard that whole year.

"I think that sounds fantastic. The children around the neighborhood could really learn a thing or two from the church to prepare them for life as an adult. Why don't you take my card and the three of us can stay in touch? I would love to work with you again Richard and perhaps see what we could do about your youth services Angela," the pastor said, handing the couple his business card.

Angela and Richard thanked him greatly. Before the three of them, including Tina, headed back towards Richard's car. Once inside, Richard dropped his calm and composed mask and wasn't afraid to show the girls his pure elation at the turn of events.

"Can you believe it?"

"It's fantastic. Wait until the rest of Angela's family back home here about this," Tina said, nudging Angela on her shoulder.

"They're going to be so proud of you," she said warmly.

Richard smiled and kissed her gently on the cheek. "Us? They're going to be proud of us, because we will do this together, you agree?" He asked. Angela smiled and nodded her head.

CHAPTER SEVEN

OUR NEW HOME

Angela found herself absorbed in her kitchen one afternoon, doing everything she could to add the perfect seasonings and herbs to the dinner she was preparing. Richard had messaged her earlier that day, stating that he wanted to come over and spend some time with her. Therefore, Angela decided it was the perfect opportunity to cook a meal for him. She felt as though it were a meal to celebrate their engagement. There were already plenty of engagement gifts piling up in her living room from close relatives and friends that had found out about their engagement.

Five minutes later, there was a knock at Angela's door, and she hurried to open it and found

Richard standing there. A bright grin was on his face. He looked more handsome than ever.

"Hello, my future wife," he said warmly.

Angela smiled brightly at him, before leaning forward to place a small and gentle kiss on his lips.

"These are for you", Richard said and handed over a gigantic bouquet that he had been carrying. Angela couldn't help but admire them with wide eyes. It was the most beautiful gift that she had ever received. He had given her an array of cardinal-red roses. It was her favorite flower, and she was overjoyed that Richard had remembered.

"Richard, they are so beautiful!" She exclaimed, rather delighted.

Richard couldn't help but chuckle at her excitement, and he leaned forward to place a soft kiss on her cheek. When he pulled back, he took in the delicious aroma that drifted through the apartment. Whatever Angela was cooking smelled delightful, and he couldn't wait to tuck into what she had prepared for them.

"It smells beautiful in here; I can tell you have been working hard all"

Angela felt warm by his praise and nodded her head, "I want you to enjoy your meal with me. Please sit down while I place these beautiful flowers in a vase."

Angela led him over to his seat around the dinner table that she had set up for them and then headed towards her kitchen to place the beautiful bunch of flowers in a glass vase that had been gifted to her by Grandma Peaches. When she placed them in the vase, she couldn't help but stare at them adoringly. Angela couldn't believe how beautiful they were. She placed the vase on the table between herself and Richard and then brought out some glasses and a bottle of sparkling cider for them to share.

"I thought we may enjoy a little glass together. I feel like I'm still celebrating," Angela said, pouring them both a glass.

"So, do I, I'm just so grateful you said yes,"

Angela was also grateful that she had agreed to marry Richard. Then again, there was never any doubt in her mind that she would have said no. Richard was the type of man that she had spent her whole life looking for. He was intelligent and kind. He had a beautiful relationship with his faith and with God and she could understand that bond between a person and their beliefs. Richard was a charitable man, and he was goal orientated. Angela knew Richard would help her in their life. He was the perfect man to raise children with and therefore she looked forward to the day she could declare him her husband in front of their church, their family, and before God.

Angela put their meal on plates and then lay the dinner down on the table. She had prepared a luscious and moist chicken dinner, complete with roasted vegetables. It was Richard's favorite meal.

"This dinner smells divine," Richard stated.

"Eat up, I have plenty more."

They peacefully ate their meal together, sipping slowly on their glass of sparkling cider. Angela always enjoyed this part of the meals they shared. Richard would always tell her about what he had been doing that day. For example, that very morning, he had been putting together scriptures that he was going to share with the church, as well as preparing the choir to perform a new song that he had composed. Richard then asked Angela about her day, and she told him how she had spent most of the day preparing for this evening. Richard had declared that he was very full by the time that he had finished his meal. However, when Angela told him she had also prepared a key-lime pie for dessert, he insisted he had enough space for that.

Halfway through their dessert, Richard had reached over the table and held on to Angela's hand. It was the hand that she wore her engagement ring on. Richard wore a small smile on his face as his finger traced gently over her engagement ring.

"I have a confession to make", Richard had suddenly declared.

Angela looked at him curiously.

"I have planned to take you somewhere this evening. Don't worry, we don't have to get all dressed up, It's just something that I have kept hidden for a while," he said. Angela found she wasn't worried at all about what Richard may have been keeping from her. In fact, she was excited to find out.

"Keeping secrets from me already, Richard?" Angela teased.

Richard chuckled and shook his head, "Don't worry my love, it is a wonderful secret."

Once they had finished their dessert. Richard helped Angela with her coat and then he drove the two of them around town. The car journey was brief, and

Angela realized she recognized the neighborhood that they were driving through. It was a very quiet and beautiful area. They were just a short walk away from their local primary school, and the church they attended was around the corner. Suddenly, the car came to a stop as Richard parked up in front of an unoccupied house.

Richard helped Angela out of the car and then looked towards the home. Angela smiled at him, but a bit confused.

"It's beautiful, but why have you brought me here?" she asked.

"Wouldn't you like to have a look inside? I think we should start looking at homes together. This one is my favorite. I would like to see what you think," Richard stated confidently.

Angela suddenly felt a thrill rush through her. She couldn't believe that Richard would start thinking about living with her in their own house together. She squealed in excitement and threw herself into his arms. The house looked grand and beautiful from the outside. It had a white picket fence wrapped around it, with a reasonably good-sized front lawn. Angela could imagine how their Christmas decorations would look like when they set them up here. There was a perfect space for a nativity scene.

"It's unfurnished, but you could imagine this place filled with our things", Richard said once he had led Angela inside of the house. She walks around the spacious living room and imagines what it would look like with a magnificent fireplace set up, the couches they would pick out together and their family portraits hanging on the walls.

The kitchen was also massive. It was almost four times the size of the kitchen at Angela's apartment. It had a clean, modern feel to it, with a large island fitted with a breakfast bar. She could imagine how it would feel to cook a thanksgiving meal for her whole family here.

"Come look upstairs", Richard said, taking her by the hand and leading her up the stairs of the house. It was a four-bedroom house. The master bedroom would be for both Angela and Richard to share. She would have a couple of spare bedrooms for whenever their friends or family would come to stay and perhaps, they could use the final spare bedroom as an office space whenever they wished to work from home. So far, everything was perfect.

"I know the upstairs of the home is wonderful, but there's one part of this home that is perfection and I want to show you", Richard led Angela downstairs to the backyard of the house. Angela was utterly elated. The house was enormous! There was plenty of space to set up a place to grow any fruit or vegetables. They would even fit the space with a firepit for those cold, winter nights.

However, Richard envisioned something else.

"I can almost imagine it now. A perfect treehouse just right there, a swing set for the children to play in. Perhaps a football net where I can teach our son to play football," he said with a wide smile.

Angela turned to look at him, full of surprise. She knew that she and Richard would eventually have a family together, but she did not know that Richard was already thinking about their future together. She smiled as bright as the sun as she could imagine it too. She could imagine their children running around in their garden, building snowmen, and making snow angels in the winter, or splashing around with the garden hose when the warm summers came around. She wanted it all too...

"I want a place to raise a family with you. I hope you would want that too?" Richard stated, watching the happy tears wail up in Angela's eyes.

"I would want nothing less!" She smiled.

They stood together side by side, looking out towards the garden. Angela had fallen in love with the vision that Richard had shared with her, and she could only imagine it happening here in this home. However, Richard may want to look at more places together, but deep down, Angela knew that her heart already belonged to this house. She looked down sadly at her feet and Richard had noticed something was wrong.

"Is something wrong?" he asked her.

"It's just... this place is perfect, it's a great location, the church is just around the corner and the local school is down the road, I think my heart lies here and I don't want to look anywhere else," she explained, looking out towards the garden.

Richard burst out laughing and grabbed her by her hand, lacing their fingers together.

"Perfect... because I have already bought the home,"

"What!" Angela screamed.

"It's ours already. I just knew this place would be perfect, and I wanted to surprise you."

Angela jumped into Richard's arms and hugged him with all her might, before running off and once again running through their empty home as she imagined all the things she could fill the house up with. Richard stared at her with a loving smile as his fiancé ran around with excitement.

"I have to take pictures to send to Grandma Peaches and we have to organize a move in date, and we certainly must have a housewarming party," Angela stated, taking as many pictures as she could.

"Anything for you,"

CHAPTER EIGHT

LIVING A DOUBLE LIFESTYLE

It had been a week since Richard had told Angela that he had secretly purchased a family home for them, and they had decided that they would move into their home right after they got married. Angela had been so excited that she wasted barely any time calling her family at home and telling them about herself and Richard had brought a house. Grandma Peaches practically cried with joy. Angela had so many things that she needed to pack up, so she hired a company to help her pack up all her belongings, therefore there were people coming in and out of her apartment all Sunday morning. Richard would have been happy to help; however, he was occupied with the church that morning. Pastor Simons of the Mega-church called him early in the morning and asked Richard for help in running the service.

Angela saw her next-door neighbor pop her head out of the door and smiled as soon as she noticed Angela standing in the corridor.

"Look like you're very busy this morning", she stated, watching as the men walked through Angela's apartment carrying stacks of folded boxes.

"Yes indeed, I apologize for the noise. My boyfriend recently proposed to me and surprised me the other week by declaring he had bought us a home," Angela said with a smile. Her neighbor jumped with excitement and ran towards Angela with her hand held out towards her.

"Oh goodness, please let me see the ring," she asked with a grin.

Angela held out her hand for her neighbor to look at. Her neighbor gasped with shock at the size of the diamond that Richard had bought her. It looked so beautiful when it dazzled in the light.

"Wow, it's beautiful. He must really care about you."

Angela nodded her head, wearing a warm smile, "He sure does".

Her neighbor looked around at all of Angela's stuff that was being packed away and then looked at the men in the room. Angela assumed she was searching for her fiancé to congratulate him on popping the question.

"Is he here to help you?"

"Not today, he's helping at our church today, I'll be heading over soon for the service,"

Her neighbor smiled and nodded her head with understanding.

"I see, we'll, I hope everything works out for you. I think I'm going to miss living next door to a kind woman," she said to Angela.

"We're going to have a housewarming party in a month. I know both myself and my fiancé would be happy to see you there?".

Angela's neighbor had happily agreed to attend their housewarming party and insisted that she would make her famous potato salad for the occasion. They had exchanged contact information to let her know the dates and time. I will be here at the apartment until after we get married. Great, her neighbor smiled. A few minutes later, the workers had finished for the morning and Angela could get ready for church.

Martha had been kind enough to pick Angela up for service to sit together like they always have.

The Sunday service went as smoothly. The pastor Simons would gather the undivided attention of the church and would read excerpts of the bible based on whatever lesson he taught that day. Richard was then called forward to deliver scriptures and Angela couldn't help but be proud of how confident he looked standing up there and speaking before the entire church. Angela looked around the church to see who had attended service and she was disappointed to see that Holly and Cameron weren't there. Ever since they had met, the couple had attended every Sunday service so far.

"I don't think you will see them for a while", Martha whispered, as she had noticed that Angela was looking around for the missing couple.

"They haven't been very discreet about their lifestyle", Martha said, referring to the couple's swinging habits. Angela couldn't help but feel disappointed. She had hoped that she had really helped them get on the right track in life and build a healthier loving bond in their marriage.

"I hoped they could integrate better into our lifestyle," she told Martha.

"Sometimes things can lead people astray in life and it's easier for them to get off track. It's up to people like us to help them find their way each time they get lost. Don't worry Angela, you can help them", Martha said with an encouraging smile. Angela smiled at her graciously. It felt nice to hear that someone other than her fiancé had faith in her. It made Angela feel more confident to set up and advice the help team within the church.

Angela sang along with the choir service that was conducted by Richard and was feeling much more positive throughout the whole service until it finally ended. Rather than go straight home, Angela had stuck around at the end of service to help with the bake sale that they put on at the end. They were hoping to raise money that would go towards repairs to the church roof and the upkeep of their beautiful stain glass windows.

After a while of steady cake sales, Angela had noticed that the church pastor and Richard were wrapped up in their own private conversation.

However, judging by the look on Richard's face, it looked as though they were discussing something rather unpleasant. Angela decided she would go over to them and make sure that everything was ok.

"If you will excuse me for a moment", she said, excusing herself before walking over to the pastor and her fiancé. Richard smiled when he saw her approaching, but there was something very awkward about the way the two men had moved from one another. It was as though they had been talking about something that they didn't want Angela to find out. Although Angela knew Richard would tell her when they were alone.

"Hello, my love", Richard said, leaning down to place a kiss on her cheek. Angela smiled at him and then smiled at the pastor Simons, holding out a hand for him to shake. He stepped forward and gave her a hug. It did not feel like the church hugs pastor Brown gave back home. Angela pulled back as pastor Simons smiled at her.

"It's lovely to see you again Pastor, hope everything has been alright?" she asked.

The pastor smiled and nodded his head.

"Don't worry about me dear, I've been getting a long alright, I assume you are very proud of your fiancé, he has always assisted me well during my services," Angela grinned at pastor Simons and then at Richard.

"I am very proud; he has learned well under your leadership,"

"You flatter me too much", The pastor said gleefully.

Suddenly, a beautiful woman walked over, along with a small child, and stood beside the pastor. Angela realized it was the pastor's wife and child. He smiled at his wife and wrapped an arm around her waist, and placed a gentle hand on his child's shoulder. Angela looked at their little family and couldn't wait to look like them one day.

"Richard, Angela, I think you both have had the pleasure of meeting my wife Cynthia and my daughter Sara," he said.

Angela smiled and leaned forward to hug his wife.

"It's a pleasure, I know I have seen you around before, but it's great to have the chance to properly meet", Angela said, after realizing that she had noticed the woman before at all the previous Sunday services.

"Indeed, it is. I've been so very excited to meet you ever since my husband mentioned that our very own Richard has finally popped the big question. You must be very excited," she said.

"I can't wait. If it were up to me, I would have him marry me in a week", Angela said enthusiastically, and the two women laughed together. Cynthia then turned to look at her husband with a loving smile.

"We know you will enjoy the married life. We will have the marriage we wish for everyone to experience," she said.

"Yes, we must get going now", pastor Simon said as he walked away. Angela noticed he appeared to look rather tense and perhaps uncomfortable with the women's conversation. He had ended their conversation rather abruptly and was in quite a rush to leave.

"Richard and I will get married and have a housewarming party soon. We would be very pleased to have you and your family attend," Angela said, extending the invite to the married couple.

"We wouldn't miss it for the world", his Cynthia said delightedly and finally the family walked away.

Once the bake sale was over, Richard walked Angela over to his car and opened the door for her like he always did before driving away. However, Angela noticed Richard was not driving her toward her apartment, but towards the town center, where most of the clubs and the bars were.

"Is everything ok Richard? does this have something to do with whatever you and the pastor were talking about before I came over?", Angela had asked once Richard had parked up in a parking lot that was across the road from the entrance to a rather empty restaurant. He nodded his head and looked upset when he turned to look at her.

"I'm afraid so. The pastor had called me over early today because it wasn't just the church that he needed help with. There are some personal issues going on and I'm afraid that the pastor isn't fit to lead us during worship anymore", Richard stated plainly. However, Angela could tell by his expression that this was hitting him quite hard. Richard had always looked up to the pastor as though he were the greatest mentor he had ever had. Therefore, whatever the pastor had done had meant that Richard had lost all faith in the man and was feeling rather disappointed.

"Please tell me Richard?", Angela pleaded.

"I think Pastor Simons has been living a double life. I don't understand why he would. You met his wife, she is a beautiful woman, she is kind, and she has faith, most of all his young child is a delight and very intelligent. I'm afraid that he isn't being faithful and seeing other women behind her back, I came here because I needed to see if it was true, if it is, then it wouldn't be fair for him to lead us during our Sunday service, he would no longer uphold the values of our church," Richard had declared.

Angela sat back in her seat, overcome with shock. This was a scandal and something that a pastor is not expected to do. She felt sorry for the pastor's wife, who probably did not know what her husband was up to, and she had seemed so thrilled earlier that day.

"Perhaps your suspicions are wrong. The pastor is a man of God. I do hope that you have gotten this wrong," Angela said.

"So, do I!"

The couple had waited in their car for up to an hour. According to Richard, he had overheard a conversation about pastor Simons planning to meet up at a restaurant with another woman. He had hoped that he had heard incorrectly. However, they finally saw the man arrive at the restaurant and he was holding the arm of a woman that they knew was not his wife.

At first, Angela wondered if maybe it was just a relative of his. However, she was proven wrong when the pastor shared a kiss with the woman that was not his wife. Angela was shocked and almost outraged that the pastor had broken his vows, however she turned to look at Richard and could see the turmoil and sadness in his eyes. She reached out and held on to his hand for support.

"I'm so sorry Richard, I know you didn't want this to be true,"

He sighed, "How am I supposed to tell his wife? She was so happy? And what about the church? What does this mean for the future of our church?".

"I'm not sure. Maybe we should still let them come to our housewarming party and you could speak to the pastor then. Get him to privately step down from his position, therefore nobody gets hurt or is publicly embarrassed," Angela suggested.

Richard nodded his head. He decided that perhaps that might be for the best.

He hoped that the church wouldn't fall apart because of this. If it did, then perhaps he could be the one strong enough to put it back together.

CHAPTER NINE:

MARRIAGE

It was a month later, and today was going to be the most important day of Angela's life. It was her wedding day, and she couldn't believe this day had finally arrived. It was what she had been dreaming about ever since she was a little girl. Angela and Tina were sitting in the bridal suite of the hotel they had booked for the night before her wedding. All her bridesmaids and her father were waiting in the hotel lobby, waiting for a glimpse of the bride. Tina was helping Angela put together the last pieces of her bridal outfit. Angela was extremely nervous and couldn't stop shaking her leg, however, she was so ready to be married.

"I can't believe how beautiful you look! I promise you Angela, when Richard sees you walking down the aisle, he's definitely going to shed some tears", Tina insisted, and she was barely holding back the happy tears in her eyes. Angela smiled warmly at her maid of honor, but she couldn't stop her leg from shaking. Tina had noticed and crouched down in front of her and held on to her hands.

"Go on Angela, I can tell when you're nervous. You have had the same nervous ticks ever since we were children. Tell me what's wrong?"

Angela chuckled. She knew Tina could read her so easily. She was grateful to have someone other than her soon to be husband that could understand her. She shrugged her shoulders.

"I don't know, it's normal to get cold-feet before the wedding. I know I love Richard and that I want to marry him and raise my family with him. I just can't believe or comprehend that we're actually getting married today and that we're going to make this commitment in front of everyone we have ever known," Angela explained.

Tina smiled at her and then helped her wipe away the tears in her eyes.

"You know you have absolutely nothing to worry about. Today is your big day, and it's going to be a day you will remember for the rest of your life. Your marriage is blessed and healthy. Besides, I might hold on to a little secret, but I'm only going to share it with you after you and Richard are declared husband and wife. Now then, let's get you in front of a mirror."

Angela laughed and then allowed Tina to help her to her feet. She thanked the make-up artists who were still in the room. Tina stood on her tiptoes as she covered Angela's eyes with her hands and walked her in front of a mirror.

"3, 2, 1..."

Tina moved away her hands and Angela froze in shock at the image before her. Angela didn't even know it was possible for her to look so beautiful. Her hair looked so elegant, tied back in a bridal bun and a veil placed in her hair. Her wedding dress was modest and elegant. The train ran back behind her and was at least 5 to 7 feet long. Grandma Peaches always said a long train means a long marriage. Angela was so overwhelmed and couldn't help but shed a few tears at the way she looked. Tina rushed forward and instantly fanned the tears out of her face.

"No, don't cry, we don't want you to smudge that beautiful make-up, come on, it's time to show Grandma Peaches and the bridesmaids your outfit," Tina said and guided her down towards the hotel lobby declaring the bride's entrance to all that were waiting.

Angela was so delighted to see her mom, Ashley and friends, Michelle, and even Martha dressed in their bridesmaid gowns. They all looked stunning. Grandma Peaches came forward and was already crying when she laid eyes on Angela in her bridal attire.

"You look absolutely amazing, my love. I can't believe that I'm alive and well to see you get married.

You have made me so very proud", Grandma Peaches said, practically wailing as she wrapped Angela up in a warm and tight hug. Finally, Angela turned to her father, and he was trying his hardest to hold back his tears as he hugged his daughter on her big day.

"You look beautiful, Richard better take good care of you,"

Angela laughed at him and then headed outside to make their way to her wedding ceremony. Her father had hired a beautiful wedding car to drive her in. Even though they had only a month to plan their wedding, a lot of money had been spent on the occasion. Their ceremony was going to take place at the mega-church that they had been invited to in the past. They would have gotten married at their own church; however, their pastor wasn't allowed to ordain the services now. The pastor at the mega-church had become great friends with Richard and insisted on marrying the couple. When they finally arrived at the church, Angela noticed that all her guests were already seated inside, waiting for her arrival.

"Let's get some pictures of the bride before she gets inside."

The photographer they had hired for the wedding had taken some pictures of Angela and her family before they entered the church and waited in the lobby for the ceremony to start. Her wedding music started to play, and their flower girls had entered, spreading around rose petals as she walked down the aisle. Spencer smiles at her, before taking her by the arm and walking Angela down the aisle. She couldn't believe how many guests had turned up for her wedding. Angela saw all the smiling faces of her friends and family as she walked by them. Richard looked at his fiancé as she walked down the aisle towards him, and he cried the moment that they locked eyes with one another.

"Who gives this woman to this man in marriage?" the pastor had said the moment that Angela had arrived at the front of the church.

"I do", Spencer said, handing her over to Richard and taking the bouquet from his daughter.

"Dear friends and family, we are gathered here today to witness and celebrate the union of this man and this woman in marriage. Through their time together, they realize their personal dreams, hopes, and goals are more attainable and more meaningful through the combined effort and mutual support provided in love, commitment, and family; and so today, before us and before God, they will begin their life together, as husband and wife."

The wedding Service went smoothly. Richard and Angela shared their vows with one another and there was barely a dry eye in the church.

"And now, by the power vested in me by the State of Atlanta, I pronounce you husband and wife. You may kiss your bride."

The newlywed couple share a kiss and the church explodes in tremendous applause. A choir sang, and Angela couldn't help but feel as though it was magical. The couple signed their marriage certificate; the image caught on camera by the photographer and before they knew it; they were traveling to their local park to take some more wedding photos before they would head towards their wedding reception.

"I can't believe I can call you my wife," Richard said.

"Neither can I, but it's official now. All we can do is to look forward to the rest of our lives together,"

Richard leaned down to place a soft kiss on his wife's lips.

"That sounds absolutely perfect to me..."

Their wedding reception was already full of guests and partying by the time the newlywed couple had arrived. Tina's speech as the maid of honor was both beautiful and the most hilarious thing she had ever heard. Grandma Peaches had also shared a few words, which had made Angela burst into tears. When all the speeches were over and the guests had been fed, the couple could share their first dance as a married

couple before dancing and singing for the rest of the

night.

"Come on, the married couple would like to cut

the cake!" Michelle declared.

Angela and Richard had cut their wedding cake

together. Everyone had taken pictures and Richard

had told everyone to go outside as he had put on a

dazzling firework display.

"I have something to tell you", Richard said

leaning in towards Angela.

"Tina spoke to me earlier; about a little secret

she had been keeping. She told me she heard the

rumors about the pastor at our church and some

people have been discussing who was going to lead

service from now on... it's me, Angela. I'm going to be

the new pastor of Ambassadors of Christ Youth Ministry,"

Angela pulled back and stared at Richard with surprise. She didn't expect the church to have decided on what was going to happen for their future.

"Is it official?", she asked.

Richard shook his head.

"Not yet. There's a church meeting in a couple of days and there will be things to discuss, but if what she says is true, this means a whole new world of opportunities will open for us."

Angela couldn't believe it. It was as though all her dreams were becoming a reality. She had just married the most perfect man on this earth and so many doors were opening for them both. She hoped it would be the beginning of an amazing future for the two of them.

"I'm happy to be with you every step of the way," Angela said, and she meant every word.

Chapter Ten: Expose

Angela and Richard had finally moved into their new home together. Most of their furniture had been delivered to their home, but they had decided that they would go shopping soon for things they would both like to have in their home. There was a lot of food cooking away in the kitchen and she would pop back inside now and then to make sure everything was going smoothly; Angela had so much going on, she couldn't help but add some finishing touches to the garden before their guests arrived for the housewarming party.

"There you are! I was wondering where my wife keeps disappearing off too," Richard said, coming out to join Angela in the garden.

She had been kneeling on the ground and arranging her new flowers in the flower bed. She looked up at him and smiled shyly.

"I'm sorry for running off. I just want everything to look perfect. You think it's beautiful enough out here? The fire pit is sent up and there's enough places out here for people to sit... did you text the DJ and ask what time he was getting here?"

Richard laughed at Angela's nervous rambling and leaned down to place an affectionate kiss on her forehead.

"Don't you worry about it, Angela. I have everything sorted out. All you have to do now is go get ready. The guests are going to arrive soon, and we have to get ready for our very special announcement,"

Angela grinned and nodded her head. They had been talking about what a beautiful wedding they had. They loved each other so much and couldn't wait any longer to start their life together. They reminisced about how their whole family had attended the wedding. The look on their faces when Angela came down the aisle ` was priceless.

"You're absolutely right! I'll go get ready now! Please keep an eye on the kitchen!" Angela yelled towards Richard as she ran inside their house to their bedroom to pick out an outfit for the night. She chose an elegant evening dress to wear. The DJ they had hired arrived only moments later and was setting up in the garden. Angela had already informed the neighbors about their celebration and had even invited them over to meet with one another. Suddenly, the doorbell rang, meaning that one of their guests had arrived early. Angela opened the door, and someone had instantly jumped into her arms.

"Angela!" they yelled. It was unmistakably, Tina.

"Tina, my goodness, you're so very early. I'm not surprised to find that you would bring some alcohol."

Tina chuckled and held up the bottles of wine that she had brought for the occasion. We do not approve of having alcohol brought to our home. Now, on an occasion, Richard and I might have wine at a wedding or a celebration. Angela looks at Tina Sternly and shook her head.

"Yes, I know you and Richard don't indulge in alcohol, but I'm certain myself and a few other guests wouldn't mind a good drink, besides I also came to surprise you nice and early", Tina chuckled and then allowed Angela to guide them around her home before coming to a stop in their kitchen. Tina was in awe at the size of their home and how beautiful the interior was.

"It just means that you can help me set everything up before everyone arrives," Angela teased.

Tina groaned and shook her head.

"Then I'm going to pour myself a drink. I think I'm going to need one" I know, I will respect your home, besides I do not drink to get drunk. "This is a special event." Tina laughed out loud!

Angela laughed at her antics and then got busy setting everything up, such as leaving her party favors by the front door. She brought out all the plastic cups and plates that would be used for the night. There was an open buffet set up in the kitchen, and there was plenty of food to go around. Michelle and her husband were next to arrive, and they had kindly brought an enormous pot of rice and peas for the guests to eat. Angela had allowed them to grab a drink and Hors d'oeuvres and get comfortable in their house as the rest of their guests trickled in.

Eventually, Grandma Peaches, Grandpa Miller, Ashley, and Spencer arrived at their home. To Angela's delight, Grandma Peaches had brought her famous sweet potato pie and her father Spencer made the best chicken ever. He was already eating his food as he walked in through the door.

The house was full of all of Angela's friends from her hometown, as well as Richard's childhood friends, their new neighbors, and their friends from church.

It was a very successful housewarming party. Richard was walking around their home introducing himself to all of Angela's friends and Angela was talking with people from her church and was putting forward her ideas for the church, such as her advice service. From what she could tell, the church members were very supportive of the idea. Suddenly, the doorbell rings and Angela answers it. She opened the door and sees that it was pastor Simons and his wife Cynthia. Angela was shocked to see him, even though she had invited them. She had almost forgotten about the sin that they had caught their pastor committing.

"Why do you look so shocked, Angela? Have you already forgotten you invited us?" the pastor teased her.

Angela chuckled awkwardly and shook her head before standing aside and letting him walk into her home.

"Of course not! I was only surprised you came; I know that you're a busy man,"

Angela didn't mean for her words to sound as though they were implying to the pastor's other activities. Thankfully, he didn't seem to notice and instead walked right into the heart of the party, leaving his wife and child at the door. Angela smiled warmly at Cynthia and offered her a hug.

"I'm so happy to see you again. I'm glad you all could make it."

"I told you we wouldn't miss this,"

Angela nodded her head with a smile and then crouched down to whisper to their young daughter, "Hello, all the other children are playing games out in the backyard. Would you like to play with them?" Angela asked kindly.

Their daughter smiled brightly at the idea of having other children to play with and instantly ran towards their backyard. Angela chuckled at how quickly she. She then stood aside and let the pastor's wife into her home, kindly taking her bag and coat and placing inside of her cloakroom.

"Please, grab yourself something to eat and drink, there's so much food here, myself and Richard are going to have so many leftovers by the end of the night,"

Cynthia smiled at Angela and passed by her to go to the kitchen and make herself a plate of food. Angela watches her walk by and can't help but feel guilty about the knowledge that this kind woman's husband was committing adultery behind her back. Angela had locked her eyes with Richard from across the room and they shared a look with one another. Richard could tell by the look in Angela's eyes that she was asking if the two of them could have a private conversation. Richard politely dismissed himself from the conversation he had been part of and walked towards Angela at the front door.

"Pastor Simons has arrived with his wife, Cynthia," she whispered.

Richard slowly nodded his head and looked down at his feet.

"I know you don't want to do this, but you have to talk with him, you can do so privately, but pastor needs to know that he is in the wrong and that he must step down from his position," Angela said softly, holding on to his arm as though to comfort him.

Richard nodded his head; he knew this was something he had to do. "I know, this is going to be the hardest thing I've ever had to do"

"I know, but I also believe in you to do what is right," Angela encouraged.

Richard and Angela were then able to get back to their party and celebrate the next step in Angela's life. She was having so much fun surrounded by her family, friends and all the new potential friends she had. Everyone was getting along well, and many people had made their way to her garden where the DJ was set up and playing their favorite songs. At one point, Angela noticed that Richard and the pastor were missing, she assumed Richard had taken him aside to have their private conversation. Angela had also noticed how the pastor's wife had been taken aside and was in a private conversation with a woman from their church. The woman was very pregnant.

Angela turned away from them and ate a piece of Grandma Peaches Sweet Potato Pie, until a glass was smashed on the ground and Angela turned to find the Pastor's wife Cynthia who was furious, she had her daughter Sara by the hand as she stomped out of Angela's house. Angela instructed the DJ to keep playing the music and then ran outside to catch up with her.

"What happened? Why are you leaving?" Angela said, holding on to Cynthia, who was shaking and visibly distraught.

"My husband has been seeing that woman from the church behind my back, she's carrying his child,"

Angela was shocked and couldn't believe what she was hearing. She knew the pastor had been seeing someone else, but she had no idea it was one of their church members and he was secretly the father to her baby. This was a huge scandal. Angela didn't know what to say to make his wife feel better, she gave her a comforting hug.

"I'm so sorry. We will do everything to support you and your child, we're going to make sure he steps down from the church, please come see me whenever you need!", Angela insisted.

His wife was grateful for Angela's kind words. Angela understood she needed to leave and take the time to process what she had learned about Cynthia's husband, Pastor Simons. Angela's heart ached for the woman; she couldn't imagine how heartbreaking it must be to find out such horrible news. Angela was able to tell Richard the news when she returned to the party and the pastor had left. They knew what must happen next, the church would have to be informed and the pastor was going to be removed from ordaining the service.

Angela started thinking and remembered her grandma Peaches had told her the church body was questioning things about years ago, but God brought a certain light on things of grave sin in the lives of the church members.

God had revealed to the servants of the Church several years prior and was attempting to stop them from acting upon their desires, but these servants fell on the fruit of the tree. These sin-seeking servants were leading others to Christ. And since the tree was not known to anyone outside the Church, God had to bring out their dirty laundry and let it be known to everyone else.

When the sin was revealed, in full view, the tree's fruit was no more, and those involved had to choose a side to stand on and repent of their sins. God had to expose the sinners to get the Church to turn back to Him. For too long, the brothers and sisters in the Church were living like the world, in sin, and doing it in God's name. The Church had to hear what happened and why those involved were removed from the church body. God is fair, and God is good. He will bring down sin to the surface and expose it. The Church had to see that there was something wrong with the church body and something had to be done. God will make a way where there seemed to be no way. God has a way of dealing with disobedience. After the sin was exposed, the church body was left to be in shame. It was a time of humbling and repentance. The Church was left to deal with their sin, which may have been a harrowing experience for some. HUMILIATION - "To make a person feel ashamed, embarrassed, or disgraced" WOW! HUMILIATION AND SHAME will be the word in the Church for a while. Perhaps this is a time for the Church to have a change of heart. The Church is in the season of humbling. *"He humbled you, causing you to hunger and then feeding you with manna, which neither you nor your fathers had known, to teach you that man does not live on bread alone but on every word that comes from the mouth of the LORD."* Deuteronomy 8:3 NIV.

HUMILIATION - Humiliation is that which causes one to feel shame or disgrace. Humiliation can be brought upon anyone, and everyone feels shame. Humiliation is not directed at just one person or one group of people. Humiliation is done to a group or even an entire community. So, on this day, God chose to expose what was hidden in the dark for so long, and the whole Church, no matter where you are, was exposed to all the eyes that were watching. *"As a result, I looked for a man among them who could build a wall. "And stand in the gap before me for the land that I should not destroy it, but I found no one. Therefore, I have poured out my indignation upon them; I have consumed them with the fire of my wrath; and I have recompensed their deeds upon their heads"* -Ezekiel 22:30-31. God Pours His Indignation Upon Them. That is what God did. When God is forced to humiliate a group of people, He pours His indignation upon them. So, what was God looking for to save from humiliation? Maybe He was looking for a few brave hearts that would stand in the gap for the Church. How does God turn the season of humiliation into one of salvation? Salvation comes when we are exposed to the wrong things in the Church, and we are forced to take a stand, one way or the other." *Salvation is of the LORD; your blessing is on your people."* -Psalms 3:8

"Because I'm about to go on a new adventure. As you can see, I've already started! Do you not see what I'm talking about? I will make a pathway through the wilderness. In the barren wasteland, I'll make rivers." -Isaiah 43:19 (KJV) (NIV). The new thing that God is doing is this. God is

doing a new thing in His Church, and he will use the faithfulness of a few. This new thing can only begin when the old thing is exposed. This new thing will only begin when the Church is forced to look at their dirty laundry. *"And he that overcomes, and keeps my works until the end, to him will I give power over the nations: And he shall rule them with a rod of iron; as the vessels of a potter shall they be broken to shivers: even as I received of my Father."* -Revelation 2:26-27 (KJV). The Overcomers are those who are faithful and Diligent in their duties. The Overcomers will be given Power and authority over the nations. The Overcomers will be given power and authority over the Churches. "To the angel of the Church in Laodicea write: "The words of the Faithful and True Witness, the Beginning of God's creation. I'm familiar with your work, and you're neither cool nor hot. I'm going to spit you out because you're lukewarm, neither hot nor cold. For you say, "I am affluent, have become wealthy, and require nothing," even though you are destitute, blind, and naked. I advise you to buy gold purified in the fire from Me, so that you may be wealthy; white robes, so that you may be dressed so that the shame of your nakedness is not revealed; and eye salve, so that you may see. *I chastise and chasten as many as I love. As a result, be zealous and repentant. I'm standing at the door, knocking. I will come in and dine with everyone who hears my voice and opens the door. And he with me. To him who overcomes I will grant to sit with me on my throne, as I also overcame and sat down with My Father on his throne."* - Revelation 3:14-21 (NKJV). Jesus comes to those who have humbled themselves. Jesus comes because of repentance. To those who have humbled themselves and repented, Jesus will come. Jesus will take those who have humbled themselves and bring them into the season of restoration. Do you have the courage to humble yourself and repent? Do you have the courage to see what sins are in your Church? Can you see what sins are in your Church? Can you see the sins are in your own life? When you observe sins in your Church or your own life, are you willing to humble yourself and repent? The process of salvation has begun. "This is the season of repentance." *"Woe to you, scribes and Pharisees, hypocrites! Because you build the tombs of the prophets and adorn the monuments of the righteous, and say, 'If we had lived in the days of our fathers, we would not have been partakers with them in the blood of the prophets.' "Therefore, you are witnesses against yourselves that you are sons of those who murdered the prophets. Fill up, then, the measure of your father's guilt. Serpents, brood of vipers! How can you escape the condemnation of hell? Therefore, indeed, I send you prophets, wise men, and scribes: some of them you will kill and crucify, and some of them you will scourge in your synagogues and persecute from city to city, that on you may come all the righteous blood shed on the earth, from the blood of righteous Abel to the blood of Zechariah, son of Berechiah, whom you murdered between the temple and the altar. Assuredly, I say to you, all these things will come upon this generation.* "*O Jerusalem, Jerusalem, the one who kills the prophets and stones those who are sent to her! How often I wanted to gather your children together, as a hen gathers her chicks under her wings, but you were not willing! See! Your house is left to you desolate; for I say to you, you shall see me no more till you say, 'Blessed is He who comes in the name of the LORD!*" Matthew 23:29-39 - (NKJV). The Church is mocked by the enemy daily. The enemy has been pounding on the door of the Church for centuries. "*For there will come a time when people will not bear sound doctrine; rather, in order to have their ears tickled, they will select for themselves instructors who will follow their inclinations, and will turn their ears away from the truth and turn aside to myths,*" mocks the enemy. 2 Timothy 4:3–4 in the New American Standard Bible

(NASB). People like to hear what they want to hear, and the Church is no exception. To meet their needs, people in the Church want to listen to all they want. What kind of praise do you want? How do you want to be praised? I can guarantee that God wants to be praised for what He has done. God does not want to be commended for the things that He has not done. The Church is filled with people who want to be honored without repentance. You must decide how you want to live. The Church is filled with hypocrites looking to hear what they want to hear. One thing that I have learned in my studies is that Jesus was not a liberal. The Church is filled with people who are liberal. The Church is filled with people who do not believe that Jesus' teachings were anything more than a set of general suggestions. People in the Church appear to believe that the Bible is a collection of thoughts and suggestions. This is not the Bible's message. This isn't the message that Jesus preached. Jesus was not a progressive. If you're a liberal, how can you be a Christian? How can you be a Christian and a conservative at the same time? How can you be a Christian and a conservative? If you are a Christian, you must be a Christian. The Bible is full of things that people do not want to hear because people like to be praised, regardless of their lifestyle and choices they make every day. Pastor Simons knew he was at fault and living a life contrary to the will and word of God. This was a private issue. Angela knew Grandma Peaches would find out sooner or later what had been prophesied and revealed, but she would not hear it from Angela. It felt wrong to end their evening on such bad news and therefore, they had told their guests that the couple was going to take on more roles in ministry.

At least their day had ended joyously.

CHAPTER ELEVEN

NEW PASTOR

Angela and Richard were both in their home that morning. They had only been living as a married couple for a day and Angela still couldn't believe that she could call herself Richard's wife. They had decided that for the time being, they would put off going on their honeymoon. There were still important matters to attend to at home and one of those things was finding out what was going to happen to Ambassadors of Christ Youth Ministry church. Angela was dressed to impress for the church meeting they had been invited to attend that way. Angela came down the stairs to find her husband pacing up and down in the kitchen, reading some notes that he had prepared. Angela couldn't help but smile at the man that she could call her husband.

"You don't have to worry about a thing, you stayed up all night preparing what to say. You already know that our church respects you. I think you're going to do perfect," Angela said confidently. Richard smiled at his wife's kind words and wrapped her up in a hug.

"I know, this is just something that I want badly for the both of us", He said. Angela nodded, she understood how important of an opportunity this was for them both. She pulled away to help him do his tie properly. Before looking off into the distance.

"Are you nervous about seeing the pastor today?" she asked. Richard nodded his head. Despite what pastor Simons had done, Richard invited him to their wedding, but he never showed up. Instead, he just appeared at his housewarming party. Richard was worried that he hated him, especially since Pastor had watched Richard grow-up within the church.

"What he did was wrong, but even God says that he can be forgiven. I just hope that he doesn't hold that much of a grudge against me. I tried to deal with him as respectfully as I could," Angela nodded her head, agreeing with him. They had really tried to deal with the pastor privately.

"You did the best you could, come on, we should go", Angela said, helping her husband into his coat and locking up their home.

Richard drove them both to their church. The church was almost silent inside, although that was because only a few people were invited to attend. They found all the guests sitting around the table. Pastor Simons was there, but he looked down at the table, refusing to make eye contact. Martha had been invited to attend, because she was the churched most frequent and longest attending member; there were also a few others that made up the church committee and of course, Angela and Richard.

"Thank you both for joining us. I also wanted to thank you for having me at your wedding. It was a most spectacular night," Martha grinned.

"Thank you so much for attending", Richard said. His words had been slightly directed at the pastor who had chosen not to attend Richard's special day. Angela and Richard took a seat next to each other.

"We all know why we are here and although it doesn't bring us much pleasure, we must discuss the future of this church and ask for the pastor to talk about his actions," a member of the church committee started to talk; however, the pastor had suddenly stood up abruptly.

"It doesn't matter, none of you need me here. It's clear that you have already decided to remove me from the church and have me replaced. I understand I must accept the consequences of my actions and will step down immediately. I only ask that you look after the people of the church and to not treat my wife as an outcast because of my actions," the pastor said, still refusing to look at any of the people sitting around the table.

Angela was feeling slightly annoyed at the pastor's attitude and his assumption that the church might treat his wife with any sort of disrespect. She shook her head.

"We will continue to offer her our support,"

Pastor Simons nodded his head at Angela's words and then turned to leave, however he was stopped by Richard who also stood up and faced towards him.

"Even if you don't lead the services anymore. I would still ask you to attend church, it's the only place to seek true forgiveness. I do not wish for you to be pushed out of this community," Richard said, showing everyone the kindness of his heart.

The pastor said nothing for a short while before he sighed and shook his head.

"I will ask God for his forgiveness in my own time, ladies and gentlemen. I wish you a good day", he said and then he left the church. The members of the church looked at one another, unsure of what to say in this situation. Richard sat back down in his seat. Angela reached out to hold on to his hand. She could understand that her husband was upset and only hoped that he would get over this situation as time passed by.

"Now that the pastor has willingly left. We must discuss who is going to lead all of our future services and what direction our church is going to head in," A woman of the committee said. Martha had smiled brightly and stood up to address the room.

"Usually, we would take a vote on this sort of situation. However, I made sure we invited Richard here today because he is the only suitable candidate for this job. He has been a follower of our church ever since he was a little boy. He completed his studies through our church, led our choir, and had been a guest at the mega-church. Richard can lead us into a great future," Martha said, smiling at Angela and then Richard, then sitting down.

The people sitting around were whispering to one another. Angela couldn't hear what they were saying, but she was certain that they were saying positive things about Richard. There was no denying that Richard had done a lot for the church, and he was possibly quite the best candidate they had. Once the whispering had died down, the eldest member of the church committee turned towards Richard.

"Do you think you are a suitable candidate to lead our church?" they asked.

Richard stood up from his seat and cleared his throat. "I have created a good relationship with everyone in our community. I have helped lead our services countless times and each time we have gone home feeling much more connected to our faith and to each other. I have countless plans for our church, and I know my wife has plenty of ideas that could also lead our youth into a brighter future,"

Angela felt her cheek flush red when the attention was brought to her, but she wanted to show them she was confident and that they could put their trust in both Richard as a pastor and Angela as the supportive wife. Richard then sat down and allowed the church committee to speak with one another before they had finally come to a decision.

"The committee has discussed this with one another in private and we have decided that Richard would be the perfect person to lead this church from now on. We want to congratulate you for becoming the

Ambassadors of Christ Youth Ministry church's new pastor,"

Richard smiled and Angela couldn't help but feel as though she was jumping for joy on the inside. There was never any doubt that Richard was going to be offered this position, but she was still extremely excited and couldn't wait to go home and share all her ideas with her husband. Richard shook hands with the church committee and one by one everyone went home until it was only Martha, Angela and Richard who were left behind. As soon as she was certain everyone was gone, Angela screamed with excitement and pounced into her husband's arms.

"I can't believe it! It's official, you are the new pastor!", she exclaimed.

Angela then pulled out of Richard's arms and jumped into Martha's arms to give her a tight hug. The elder woman simply laughed at her.

"Thank you so much for your kind words and influence. I know Richard will lead the church much more efficiently." Angela smiled.

Martha laughed and shook her head, "Don't worry, I completely believe in your husband, and I am very much looking forward to the ideas and classes that you could bring to the church. I think you might improve our Sunday school classes for the children."

Angela nodded her head enthusiastically. She already had so many things she wanted to implement into the Sunday school classes and now that her husband was the church's new pastor, she could do all the things she dreamed of doing. Martha stuck around for a little while to talk with the married couple before deciding that she ought to get home. Angela grinned and held her husband in her arms as soon as they were the only people left.

"I knew you could do it," she whispered in his ear. Richard didn't say anything in return, but Angela knew he was ecstatic.

"Look at this place, this is your church now Richard, everyone believes in you, and I believe in you too,"

Richard smiled, believing that with Angela's support, he could do anything.

CHAPTER TWELVE

SIN'S DISCOVERED

The church was halfway through its Sunday service, and it was Richard who was leading his very first service by himself. When the church had found out what their old pastor had done, many of the members were left disappointed and understood the reasons the old pastor had been dismissed. However, they were reacting positively to the way Richard was leading his service. Even Angela's friend Michelle and her husband visited the church. Richard's first service as the church's pastor. At the end of service, Angela was left to run her first Sunday school session. Once she was done with the children, she would leave her door open for any adults that may seek advice.

Angela paced around the room and looked at all the colorful drawings that the children were making. Earlier in the session, she asked the children to draw what God meant to them. Angela came to a stop in front of the old pastor's daughter. Much to Angela's delight, the old pastor's wife Cynthia and their daughter Sara continued to go to church. She was happy to see the church was treating them with kindness and was helping her through her difficult time. Angela kneeled to look at the child's drawing.

"This is beautiful, does your mother know that you are quite the artist?" Angela praised.

The little girl nodded with pride.

"My mom says that she loves it when I draw, she puts all of my drawings up on our fridge."

Angela smiled at her and then read what she had written about God. The little girl had written, 'God means forgiveness'.

"This is what God means to you?" Angela asked softly, pointing towards what she had written. Sara smiled shyly and nodded her head.

"I know mommy is angry with daddy, but I remember reading somewhere that God is forgiving, and I know they can forgive one another. I know our house can be happy," Angela smiled at the child's positive outlook. However, she still felt bad about what she may be going through. She didn't want to pry into Sara's home life to know what was going on at home. Angela knew that what was happening must be difficult on a small child, and yet the little girl was still wearing a radiant smile on her face.

Angela walked around the room more, inspecting all the drawings. She then noticed that someone was standing by the door. When she looked up, she was very surprised to find that Holly and Cameron were standing there, waiting to speak with her. Angela checked the time and realized that it was the end of Sunday school.

"Alright children, that is the end of Sunday School, and I am so very delighted at all the work you have done this evening. If you haven't finished, you can take your drawing home with you. If you have, just place your drawing at the front of my classroom and tidy up after yourselves before you find your parents," she said before dismissing her class.

Angela had helped clear up the arts and craft materials as she waited for each child to leave the room. After all the children left, she invited Holly and Cameron to the room. "Make sure you closed the door behind you." The couple sat down across from Angela. Cameron failed to meet her eyes, and Holly appeared to be very embarrassed. Despite their recent absence, Angela was still happy to see them.

"Holly, Cameron, I have to admit, I wasn't expecting to see you both again. I thought you had left our church for good," Angela stated.

"We tried really hard, we wanted to connect, we felt as though the only people who was giving us a chance was yourself and your partner Richard," Holly said, looking down at the table as though she was too ashamed to meet Angela's eyes.

"He's my husband now,"

Cameron and Holly then gave her a bright grin, "Oh wow, congratulations. I hope Richard knows how lucky he is."

Angela smiled, grateful for their kind words. "What happened? Everything was going so well?", she asked.

Cameron sighed, "You have to understand. Holly and I have been living the way we have for a very long time. We thought we could give up swinging easily, but we gave in to a moment of weakness and started to see other married couples again, only this time we weren't taking as much care as we usually do."

Angela knew the couple had most definitely fallen back into their old habits when they had missed many services. Although, she was unsure what they may have been referring to this time.

"I caught herpes", Holly suddenly declared.

Angela knew it was a sexually transmitted infection, caught through unprotected sex, and then it started to make sense why Holly and Cameron had been too embarrassed and too ashamed to come to church.

"Have you gone to seek medical help?" Angela asked.

The couple didn't say anything. Angela knew what that meant.

"We're too embarrassed, and we don't want to explain why this has happened or have the doctors to judge us. We just want to get better, and we don't know how to do it," Holly declared.

Angela sighed; she wasn't quite sure what to do in this situation. This was something completely new that she had never dealt with before. She knew that there were other churches that would shun Holly and Cameron and turn them away. Angela didn't want to turn them away. She was not going to give up on them. Angela wanted to show them that God could lead them down a brighter path if they are willing to let him in their lives.

"The doctors have seen many medical emergencies during their careers. Believe me when I say they will not judge you, but you must seek professional help, so it will not spread to your partner... I also want you to know that the church will still keep its doors open to you," Angela told them.

Cameron and Holly's eyes widen in shock as they shook their head. They were prepared for Angela to turn them both away. Holly and Cameron wasn't expecting her to show them such kindness, especially since they had turned their backs on her the last time she had tried to help. "Seriously? Angela, even after what we have done. You kindly invited us into your church, but we gave in and went back to the lifestyle that we knew"

Angela nodded her head and smiled at the couple.

"I can understand that. It doesn't matter if I disagree with your lifestyle, because I can still understand that people have come from different walks of life than I have. It's hard to give something up completely own your own, but by coming to see me today proves the two of you are really trying to be better for yourselves, that is what you want, isn't it? To learn to stop swinging and connect with the church?"

They nodded eagerly, "More than anything"

"You know bible says that you should owe no one anything, except to love each other and that love is patient and love is kind. The bible can help guide you towards a loving and faithful marriage. You just have to believe in yourselves to commit to this church and trust in me to help guide you."

Holly and Cameron looked at each other and smiled as they held on to each other's hand. Angela could see the love and trust they shared, she just wanted to open their eyes and show them they only needed each other.

"My husband Richard now leads this church; His service may be of better help for the two of you. I also stay after service to run the Sunday school and an advice service; you are both always free to find me and talk about any of your worries."

The couple nodded and then stood up before shaking Angela's hand.

"Thank you, Angela, for believing in us," Holly said.

"I hope I will see you both at next week's service?", Angela asked.

"Absolutely!"

They said before leaving. Angela could tell by the determination on their faces that she would see them both in next week's service. A few minutes later,

Richard knocked on the door to announce his presence and walked into the room.

"Was that Holly and Cameron I just saw walk by?"

Angela nodded her head.

"They had fallen back to their old lifestyle. I think they came here looking for my forgiveness and for advice,"

"That, my dear, is why we have God,"

Angela smiled and nodded her head. It was indeed why they had God. She knew God had a plan, not just for herself and Richard, but for all those who would seek his guidance.

CHAPTER THIRTEEN

TREATMENT

Angela rose in the morning feeling incredibly refreshed and ready to start the day. It was a Sunday, which was her favorite day of the week. Richard was planning something special for the church to do and so the church wouldn't be open for regular service that day. However, Angela had planned to continue her advice services and had invited Holly and Cameron to come along later in the day, she had a surprise planned for them and she hoped they would be thankful for it. The sun was shining brightly, and its beams of light seeped through the blinds, landing on the peacefully sleeping body of her husband. Angela still couldn't believe that she could call herself a married woman to a man who will share her love and ideals for the rest of their lives. Grandma Peaches and her mother had called the married couple earlier that week to check up on them and see how blissful they were in their new marriage. Angela was grateful to have such a loving and supporting family.

Angela slowly got out of bed, making sure not to disturb her husband who was peacefully dreaming and had already gotten dressed for the day. Just as she was about to leave, she could hear Richard stirring in his sleep before sitting up and smiling at her lovingly.

"You were going to leave without kissing your husband goodbye?", He asked playfully.

Angela chuckled before walking towards him and placing a light kiss on his lips, "I'm sorry my love, I didn't want to disturb you, you looked so peaceful, it would have been such a shame to pull you out of your slumber."

"Are you going to church?"

Angela nodded her head, "Yes, I have a few people that wanted to see me today, I know that some of our church members are going through such a difficult time and so I wanted to make sure they felt like they were being heard."

"What did I do to deserve such a kind wife?"

Angela blushed brightly at Richard's praise. "You deserve everything, I must tell you every day what a good man you are."

Richard chuckled before laying back down in bed.

"I've actually invited Holly and Cameron to see me this evening," Angela told him.

"Really?" Richard asked, appearing curious. Richard had spent little time talking to the married couple, although Angela had told him everything about them and he knew how much his wife wanted to build a good relationship with them. Richard knew she was hoping to show them how good it was to lead a happy Christian lifestyle.

"Yes, I told you they had come to me last week with worrying news about their health. It saddened me to see how lost they seemed, they had no clue where to start, so I thought I could help them take the first steps." Angela told him. Richard nodded approvingly, before wishing his wife goodbye and letting her make her way to their church.

At church, Angela had been approached by a few married couples who had wanted advice about their marriage and how to be good help mates in their household. Angela had only been married for a couple months, but she was happy with her relationship and really tried her best to advise the couples on how to be content in their marriage and to always refer to the word of God whenever they felt as though they were being led astray. This was also an opportunity to build better communication with the members of the church. Ever since the scandal that had come out about the previous Pastor, Angela had noticed that many members appeared to be discouraged about coming back to service in their church and were untrusting. However, by being helpful, honest, and open with the members, Angela and Richard were building trust and friendly relationships with the church and the community. Angela had also invited some children in the church to her sessions, she wanted their advice on what they would love to learn about in Sunday School and what activities they would like to do. For example, many of the children were excited about the idea of creating and performing plays based on stories from the bible to perform for the church. She thought that if the children were having fun at church, it would encourage learning and inspire the youth to follow a good Christian life.

Angela was in the middle of discussing these ideas when she noticed Holly and Cameron were waiting by the door.

"Thank you so much for coming today children, I love all the ideas you have given me, they are absolutely fantastic, and I will make sure we use some of these in our next sessions. You can all go home now and enjoy the rest of the day and I look forward to seeing you again in next week's Sunday school," Angela dismissed the smiling children and then invited Holly and Cameron into the classroom once it was clear.

"Hello to you both, I'm thrilled you could clear your schedules to see me today", Angela smiled, pulling Holly into a friendly hug, and shaking Cameron's hand before showing them to their seats.

"We're both really grateful that you invited us here today. We were unsure if the church wanted anything to do with us... we really thought that we were beyond saving," Holly admitted.

"Nobody is beyond saving. I'm unsure whether I have said this already, but I will not give up on you", Angela admitted. Holly and Cameron smiled warmly at Angela. They have never had a friend that had shown them as much care and concern as Angela did. It was enlightening and really gave them hope.

"There is a reason I actually invited you here today. I remember you telling me about your health issues Holly, and I know you were unsure about what actions to take next. I wanted to take you both to the clinic today. I know you feel too embarrassed to see a doctor about your herpes, but you can't leave these things untreated. I will take the two of you there today if you let me?" Angela asked them.

Holly turned to Cameron with a questioning gaze. They appeared to be uncertain whether it was something that they wanted to do.

"Would you be willing to stay with us? I know you don't owe us anything Angela, but I think it would really make me feel better if I knew I had someone, other than my husband, to be there and support me?"

"Absolutely, I'd be more than happy to."

The three of them agreed to let Cameron drive them towards the clinic, with Angela giving them directions. The clinic was rather empty when they arrived, with only a couple of people sitting in the patient waiting area. Angela had told Holly what to say to the receptionist before the three of them had taken seats and waited for Holly to see the doctor. A doctor emerged only a few minutes later and had called their names. Angela told them she would wait in the waiting area for them, because she wanted the couple to have their privacy. She made herself a nice, hot cup of coffee as she waited and placed a few pamphlets about the church on the side for people who were interested in reading and attending if they chose to. A half an hour had passed by before Holly and Cameron had emerged. The smile on Angela's face had dropped when she saw panic in Cameron's eyes and Holly's face was drained of all color, appearing as white as a sheet.

"What happened? Is everything ok?" Angela asked. Holly didn't say anything as she froze in shock.

"I think it would be best if we spoke about this in the car", Cameron said, guiding the two women out of the clinic and letting them get settled in the car.

Holly had suddenly burst into tears and appeared to be inconsolable. Angela tried her best to soothe Holly's pain by helping her get her breathing under control so that she could tell Angela what was wrong.

"Please tell me what is wrong, it hurts me to see you so upset."

"Would you like the good news or the bad news first?" Cameron asked her.

"The good news, please."

"The good news is that we told the doctor about Holly having herpes. She was a very respectful doctor, and she told us we didn't have to be embarrassed and that it was a good thing that we had come to her because she offered Holly treatment to get it all under control," Cameron said.

Angela let out a breath of relief and was happy for them until she realized they had other news to share.

"And the bad news?", She asked.

"I'm pregnant!", Holly shouted before covering her face with her hands.

"You're pregnant, and both of you are upset by that? Forgive me, but I don't understand, a baby is a blessing", Angela told them. She wanted to sympathize with the couple, but Angela thought that the news about Holly carrying a new life was the best thing anyone could hear.

"We understand we are married and so having a baby would appear to be the next natural step in our lives. However, me and Holly had always said we didn't want to have any children, we wanted to focus on our work and travel the world. I didn't think I would be a good dad and we have absolutely no idea how to look after a baby, let alone raise one," Cameron explained.

"I'd be a terrible mother," Holly croaked sadly.

"You know, it is possible to live the life you want, to see the world and look after a baby. It may seem to be difficult at first, but everyone who has their first baby doesn't know where to start. I understand you may feel lost, but I have a feeling the two of you will be natural," Angela advised them, hoping that she could show them how beautiful a gift they had been blessed with and not be afraid of the future.

"I could always have an abortion," Holly stated.

Angela couldn't help but frown. Angela understood it was always the mother's choice to choose whether they would keep and raise their child. Her upbringing and teachings from Grandma Peaches, taught Angela abortions were an option to be avoided, she believes children are a gift from God. Jesus Christ values all life and wants his children to share their love with all, born and unborn. Angela really wanted to open Holly and Cameron's eyes to this revelation.

"I cannot force you both to do anything. I would never take away your choice, but as a friend please let me advise you. It is the way of the Lord to love all his children, including your unborn child. I see the love you have for each other, and I can see your fear. I know this was something you were completely unprepared for, and you don't know where to start. I know in my heart that the two of you would love this child unconditionally. I will never allow you to struggle. The church will always be there for you both every step of the way. I think we should all go home now, and you can take your time to think about what I have said," Angela suggested.

Holly rubbed away the tears from her red, puffy eyes and nodded her head. Cameron had also agreed, and the couple appeared to be in better spirits.

Three months had passed since that day. Holly and Cameron had informed Angela the week after they found out Holly was pregnant; they wanted to keep their baby and raise a family. Every week for the past three months, Holly would meet Angela during her advice and would keep her up to date about the pregnancy and how she was tackling living with herpes. Angela could see that she was becoming more and more stressed every week and she did everything she could to help her relax.

Unfortunately, Holly came to Angela one evening with devastating news. Holly had lost her baby because of stress. Angela held Holly in her arms as she cried for the baby she never got to meet. Angela couldn't help but cry with her, feeling her pain. She hoped that the baby's soul was at rest in the arms of their God. Holly and Cameron had bonded closely through their pain and had attended church more frequently, finding God through their loss by asking for forgiveness and a path to guide their way.

They declared that they willingly wanted to dedicate their lives to the church and to God.

CHAPTER FOURTEEN

ACCEPTING CHRIST

Today was an important day for the church. Over the past week, Angela and Richard had invited Holly and Cameron to their home to discuss how they were going to transition into a happy, Christian life as well as providing the couple with emotional support as they were still going through the pain of losing a child. Holly and Cameron were going to declare their dedication in front of the whole church during an altar call. They had thought long and hard about it, had left behind their swinging lifestyle and was ready for a new adventure. Angela was sitting beside Martha at the front of the church, and they talked with one another while Richard was setting up the service dedicated to Holly and Cameron. Martha was one of Angela's closest friends in the church. She was much older than Angela, with adult children and grandchildren of her own. Angela smiled warmly at her as she talked to her about her oldest child being blessed with pregnancy and she was so excited to be gifted with another Grandchild, furthermore her youngest child had graduated the top of her class and Angela was so happy to see the glee that family brought to Martha. Angela couldn't wait to have a family of her own. She wanted the joy of bringing a child into the world and to watch them grow up into a fine, handsome, or beautiful man or woman.

Martha and Angela were in the middle of their conversation when Holly and Cameron came to sit beside her. Angela turned towards them with a grin and could see the excitement on their faces.

"I'm so happy to see you both. Today is your big day. You get to declare your dedication to God In front of the whole church. "How are you feeling?", Angela asked, reaching over to pull Holly into a comforting hug.

"We are both incredibly excited, we didn't think that either of us would ever get a chance like this in our lives. We have lived a certain way for so long. I think we're both excited to see how much our life can change for the better after today," Holly said, holding onto Cameron's hand for his love and support.

"We already told our family. They were surprised that this was the path me and Holly were going to take, but they were happy to support us and said they would be with us every step of the way. We are so ready for this," Cameron stated.

Angela nodded her head with a bright grin, her family had grown up in the church, so she understood how important it was to have family that would support her religious beliefs and her choices, Holly and Cameron were going to have an easy integration within the community, especially with their family's support. "I'm happy for you. I also think that you are going to have fun within the community, especially if you have a much more hands-on approach, you could start helping us with the church bake-sales after service, perhaps you could help me with a few Sunday school sessions whenever you feel up to the challenge?".

Holly nodded her head eagerly, "Thank you so much Angela... for everything,"

"You're welcome,"

Finally, the service had started, and Richard had delivered the sermon as he usually did. Angela loved how passionate he was whenever he was leading service. Sometimes it was as though God spoke through him. Richard was inspiring, and he engaged with each one of the church members. In the middle of his sermon, Richard mentioned the people who had dedicated their life to Jesus, showing that he was about to start altar call. "In just a few minutes, I am going to give you a chance to decide to follow Jesus", He told them. Holly and Cameron turned to look at one another with bright smiles, and the invitation was coming, and they were eager to take it.

"I want all those who are considering giving their lives to Jesus to decide, I ask will you choose to reject him or will you choose to embrace him in your lives, Moses had plainly set out the choices himself, he says 'I have set before you life and death, blessing and cursing; therefore choose life', Deuteronomy 30:19, and so I must ask you members to choose life." Richard says and opens his arms out to the church. He points to his altar and invites those who wish to accept the invitation to give their lives to Jesus. Angela turned towards Holly and Cameron with an encouraging smile. The couple had made their choice long ago and were eager to leave their seats and approach the Altar to show that they chose the blessing.

Angela had to hold back the tears in her eyes as she watched Holly and Cameron give their lives to God in front of the church. She was incredibly proud and honored to bear witness to their dedication. She knew this meant help, blessing, and healing would open to them both. Once Alter call was over, Holly and Cameron returned to their seats and were congratulated by the church on the way back to their seats. The choir had burst out into song, their beautiful, angelic voices almost raising the roof with the church singing and dancing with them.

Angela turned towards Holly and Cameron during the choir's song.

"I hope both of you can stay a little longer after church, I know many of our church members would like to personally congratulate you. Richard and I may also have a surprise for you if you are not busy for the rest of the day?" she asked.

"We aren't busy, we would be happy to stay."

As promised, Holly and Cameron stayed behind at the end of church and were approached by many people who wanted to thank them and congratulate them for taking Jesus into their lives.

Angela and Martha stood back to watch them with a smile on their faces. Angela could see how happy Holly was, and how much more support she was going to have as they got through their difficult time. She waited until the crowd had died down a little before approaching the couple herself and pulling them into a tight hug. "Tell me, how are you both feeling?".

"It was a little nerve wrecking walking up to the Altar, knowing that everybody's eyes were on us. But once we were up there, all our nerves went away, and I felt a genuine connection. It is normal to feel such a strong pull?" Holly asked.

Angela nodded her head with a knowing smile, "Absolutely, that pull, that connection, brings all of us together in church every week. I am amazed you can both feel that. I can't wait to be with you for the rest of your journey. Thank you both for listening to me the day we met and for turning up."

"Thank you for approaching us, and not turning away once you found out about our sins," Cameron said, placing a friendly hand on Angela's shoulder.

Richard had finally emerged from the church and approached his wife and her friends. He smiled at them, before standing beside Angela and wrapping a hand around her waist, "Well done to you both today, this is a great start for you. Has my lovely wife told you her surprise yet? I was hoping I hadn't missed that part", He said, smiling down at Angela.

"Not yet, but I'm about to", she chuckled, before looking at Holly and Cameron who were very eager to hear what Angela had prepared for them.

"I hope the two of you have an appetite. I love a good excuse to cook, so I and Richard wanted to throw a celebratory meal for you at our home. Martha and a few of your other friends you met in church are coming along. We just thought that it was a joyous occasion and something that needed to be celebrated," Angela explained.

Holly and Cameron were impressed and couldn't believe that Angela and Richard would do such kind things for them.

"Absolutely, we would love to come over! I can't believe you both have done this for us," Holly exclaimed.

"Of course, we better get going. I can already hear my Husband's stomach growling", Angela teased. The group of friends laughed at each other, before heading towards their own vehicles and making their way to Angela and Richard's home.

The celebratory meal at Angela's home was home baked bread, which smelled divine and had given Richard an excuse to show off his bread-making skills, which Martha had heavily praised him for. There was also a serving of garden veggies that had been grown in their garden by Angela herself, and she made sure her veggies were gently roasted and drizzled in old balsamic vinegar. A succulent chicken was prepared. It was beautifully moist and was adored by Holly and Cameron, who had gone back for seconds. Their friends were joyful, and shared some terrible jokes, courtesy of Richard's sense of humor and overall welcomed and celebrated Holly and Cameron's new start. During the meal, Holly had stood up at the table with a small glass of sparkling cider in her hand and had insisted on sharing a speech.

"First, I would like to say a huge thank you to you all for being here and letting me know myself and my husband will have your support and your good blessings as we live the new life the both of us deserve. I must thank Angela, who has been our very own guardian angel. When Angela approached myself and my husband, she did not judge us, nor did she turn her back on us. She showed us that there is a better way to live, a way that could bring us happiness, especially after the dark couple of weeks we have had with the loss of our child. We need good Christian women like Angela in our lives. I only hope that one day I could be like her. So, I wish to drink to Angela, to friendship, and to the church," Holly said, holding her glass up as everyone around the table cheered and knocked their glasses together.

The celebration ended in the late evening. Holly and Cameron were the last ones to leave. They thanked the couple one last time for their hospitality and support before going home. Angela and Richard flopped down on their couch with exhaustion. Once all the guests had gone home. They were full of great food and were happy to have such an evening go by smoothly.

"I guess I should make a start with doing the dishes", Richard said, looking over at the pile of plates by the side. Angela looked over at them and laughed.

"I think we owe it to ourselves to wash them in the morning. We are both exhausted and deserve an early night. Though we should wrap up all the leftover food and put it away in the fridge", She said, getting up from the couch and putting all the excess food into Tupperware. Richard stood beside her, helping her put everything away. However, Angela started to feel rather nauseas and stopped for a moment to collect a glass of water, she hoped it wasn't the food that was making her ill. "Is everything alright my love? You're looking rather pale", Richard said, placing a hand on her forehead to feel whether she was coming down with a fever. Angela shook her head and poured herself another glass of cold water. "I'm sure everything is fine. I might have eaten a little too much or perhaps had too much cider", Angela said, brushing it off. She went to bed and hoped that whatever it was would be gone by the morning.

CHAPTER FIFTEEN

BLESSINGS

Angela woke up hesitantly that morning. She tried to get out of her bed, but her muscles felt heavy with fatigue and ached whenever she tried to move it. She had a slight headache, but her stomach was gurgling and hurt. For a moment, she was worried that she had caught some sort of terrible illness, or maybe it was the food that she had prepared the night before. If that was the case, she would be mortified. After all, she had served that food to all her friends. She wanted to get out of bed and use the house phone to check in on everyone to make sure that everyone was feeling alright. However, she was worried that the minute she sat up, she would spew all over the bathroom floor. Richard walked into the bedroom, smiling brightly, and dressed immaculately, ready to do some work for the church. He approached the bedroom windows and threw the curtains to let in all the sunlight, "It's such a beautiful day outside, it's not good for you to sit in bed, in the darkness all day", He teased, sitting down on the edge of the bed. Angela groaned loudly and turned to bury her head in the pillow to block out the offending rays of light.

"Angela, is everything alright my love?"

Angela shook her head and held on to her stomach, "No, I feel absolutely terrible this morning. Is there any chance you could grab me a glass of water and two Tylenol?" she asked him. He nodded his head and left for just a moment, before quickly returning and giving his wife what she had asked for.

Angela took the painkillers and washed it down with water to soothe her dry mouth.

"I'm afraid I feel terrible this morning, Richard. I know you were looking forward to me helping you out with your work today, but I'm going to throw up the minute I get out of bed. Could you please call everyone that had dinner here last night and make sure that they are all ok?", She asked him.

Richard nodded his head and ran a comforting hand through her hair. "Of course, I will. But I'm not sure if it was the food. I thought it was prepared and cooked properly. I also ate the food and I feel perfectly fine. However, I don't mind staying home to look after you today. I'll prepare you a light breakfast with hot lemon water," Richard said, leaning down to press a light kiss on her forehead.

As soon as he left the room, Angela jumped out of bed, running as quickly as she could to the bathroom. She made it just in time to throw up in the toilet. She couldn't remember the last time she had felt this ill; it was probably when she was a little girl and had come down with a stomach bug. However, Angela couldn't help but feel like something was different about this illness. She tried to think about what it could be; she was very hygienic, and Richard was right, he had eaten the food and he was perfectly fine.

Richard had walked into the bathroom and found his wife clutching the toilet bowl. He lowered himself to the ground beside her and comfortingly rubbed her back, "I've spoken with everyone who was here last night, and they told me they are perfectly fine, so I wouldn't worry about it being the food", He said. Angela sighed, grateful that she hadn't accidentally given all their guests' food poisoning. She then sat back and really thought about it, she had been having these random bouts of queasiness at odd times in the morning, and a few cramps. Angela thought they were just signs that her time of the month was approaching.

Her time of the month never arrived, though.

In fact, she was late.

"What is it, Angela?" Richard asked, noticing Angela's dazed look.

"Richard, I'm going to need you to go to the store and buy me a few pregnancy tests," Angela said.

Richard's eyes widened with shock, before nodding his head, "Do you really think you could be?" He asked, placing his hand on her stomach. Angela shrugged, she was hopeful, but she couldn't be sure until she found out for sure. Richard quickly gathered his keys and left the house in search of a test. Richard returned in record-speed time and allowed Angela the privacy of taking the tests alone.

The wait for the results felt like forever. While she waited for the results, Angela paced up and down the bathroom and thought about what she would do depending on the results of the test. If it was negative, she would be a little disappointed and so would Richard, but that also meant that they would have more time to prepare for a baby and spend more time furthering their careers. If it was positive, that would mean that a baby would arrive in less than nine months' time, and that seemed like a tiny amount of time to prepare to bring a new life into the world. She knew Richard wanted children; they dreamed of a family together, and she would be so happy to be pregnant, but she was also scared about how to prepare for a baby.

It was time to look at the results and read the results... Positive

Angela yelled out in joy and ran out of the bathroom to where Richard was sitting on the bed waiting. He took one glance at the wide grin on his wife's face and knew straight away what the result was. "We're having a baby, aren't we, Angela?" He asked, pulling his wife into a tight hug. Angela nodded her head, with happy tears streaming down her face. "Yes, we are, can you believe it Richard, we're going to raise a baby of our own, we're finally going to have our own family", She told him.

That beautiful future that Angela had always wished for was now becoming a reality.

CHAPTER SIXTEEN

WORKER'S LIFE

Angela sat at her dining room table. She was surrounded by baby books, magazines, and articles. She couldn't wait to get stuck in and find out what she would have to do to prepare to be a mother. She read all about what type of food was good to eat at the beginning of her pregnancy, compared to what it would be good to eat at the end. She read all about where to buy the best baby clothes, cribs, toys, everything that she would need to have before she gave birth to a beautiful little boy or girl. She was just so excited to be a mother and to raise a child here in the home that Richard had chosen for them. She called her mother, father and Grandma Peaches, the moment she had found out that she was pregnant, and she was unsurprised by the range of reactions. But one thing that was clear was that her family supported them and couldn't wait for a new addition to arrive. Richard walked into the room, carrying a laptop in his hand. He bent down and placed a light kiss on his wife's lips.

"Good morning to my beautiful wife, and the mother of my child", Richard said with a loving grin, his eyes flickered down to Angela's flat stomach. Richard had also informed his own family. His father was happy to hear the news, but his mother had been ecstatic and couldn't stop crying on the phone. Richard was her only child and therefore she was so overjoyed to be given her first grandchild.

"Good morning, what is all this you are looking very busy for this time of day?" Angela said, pointing towards his open laptop.

Richard shrugged his shoulders. "I have been looking around on some job websites. I love being pastor at our church. But I have so much free time between my time here and my duties at church. If we include the fact that we have a baby on the way, I think it would make sense for me to get another job. There's a job listing here for a computer engineer at Apple. It's highly aspirational, but I know I'm qualified to do it." he said, turning his laptop around so Angela could read over the job listing.

"I think it's a wonderful idea Richard, I do. But do you think you would really have the time? I don't want you to get overwhelmed."

"I know I have the time; we're going to need all the financial help we can get. Just think, Diapers and milk powder don't come cheap these days. We also must think about healthcare and a school fund on top of that... I really want this job. I just need a little help with putting my resume together," Richard admitted, pulling up the resume he had been working on. Angela sighed and then handed him her mobile phone.

"Here, ring Spencer, he knows all about it."

"I'm sure he wouldn't mind talking with you and advising you on what to write, if you ask him kindly enough, he may even go to the job interview with you she told him with a smile. After all, you used to be his assistant." He nodded his head and accepted her advice.

"Thank you! I'll keep you updated with everything", Richard promised before disappearing upstairs to ask for Spencer's advice.

Angela sighed as she watched her husband walk away, before turning back to her magazines and making a note that she ought to book an appointment with the Doctors, so they could advise her with the next steps of her pregnancy. She couldn't wait for her first ultrasound and couldn't help but imagine Richard's face as he stood beside her, listening to their baby's heartbeat.

Spencer had been happy to receive Richard's call and offered him advice about how to arrange his resume, such as making sure that he included all relevant work experience with legitimate references. His personal statement had to be a great reflection of the type of worker Richard was. Thanks to Spencer's help, Richard received an email almost two weeks later, inviting him to an interview for the job. It had been a long time since he last attended and interview for a job, therefore he took Angela's advice and had asked Spencer if he would be willing to come to the interview with him and offer him some advice and perhaps the two of them could grab some lunch together afterwards.

"Angela, come on, come give your father a hug", Spencer said as he arrived at Angela's home to collect Richard for his interview. Angela grinned and ran up to her father, letting the man pull her into a warm hug.

"How have mom and Grandma Peaches been since I told you all the great news?", Angela asked.

"Your mother had barely stopped crying about it. You wouldn't believe how excited she is for a baby to enter the family. Your Grandma hasn't stopped knitting onesies and tiny hats ever since she found out", Spencer chuckled, and Angela shook her head fondly. Richard walked down the stairs, wearing a steam-pressed suit, looking elegant and clean-shaven. He approached Angela and held out a hand for Spencer to shake.

"Thank you so much for coming with me, sir."

Spencer took his hand and shook it firmly, "Thank you for making me a grandfather, well, we'd better get going, we'll see you later Angela", Spencer said and waited outside in the car for Richard.

"Wish me luck", Richard said kissing her gently on the cheek before heading towards his interview.

Richard came back that evening, feeling certain that he had done a good job. He remained calm and answered all the questions to the best of his ability. Angela and Richard found it to be an extremely long wait before they would find out. Angela really hoped that Richard would get the job, she could see how much this meant to him, but as time passed, they thought they would not be contacted because someone else had been offered the position. Suddenly, the email they were waiting for had arrived. Richard was given the position.

CHAPTER SEVENTEEN

MONSTER-IN-LAW

I must say, this is the best idea I have ever had,"

Tina said. Angela couldn't help but agree.

Angela had met up with her cousin that morning. She

had a lot of free time and realized that she and Tina

hadn't spent as much time together as they usually did.

Tina noticed Angela had been rather stressed and a

little tense ever since she had found out she was

excited. Angela was ecstatic to be carrying a baby and

starting a family with Richard. However, she didn't

realize how much preparation was included when

getting ready to bring a baby into the world. Therefore,

Tina had suggested they both went to a yoga class

together, to stretch and perhaps do a little mindfulness.

It was a very relaxing environment, the class took place

in a little studio in town and was playing calm,

classical pieces of music as the women stretched and meditated on the mats beside each other. "I have to admit, this really was a great idea, Tina. I really needed to be in a peaceful environment. I love being at home with Richard and he has been a very supportive husband, but I also know he's been busy with church and his new job on the side", Angela said, as she stretched and got into the warrior pose. I can't do every pose because some of them are not of God. They are Buddhist poses worshiping a different God. We must be careful. I am glad you are here with me. I do need to stretch Angela winked at Tina.

"Sometimes you need someone other than your husband to talk to and it's my job as your loving cousin to make sure you are having a calm and happy pregnancy," Tina said with a grin. Angela chuckled at her and nodded her head.

"Aren't I so lucky", Angela teased, reaching over to take a cooling sip from her bottle of water.

"I have to ask you about it, though. I just can't believe that you're pregnant. It's strange seeing someone that I grew up with, carrying a child of their own. In fact, it makes me feel as though we're getting old," Tina laughed. "How did Ashley, Spencer, Grandpa Miller, and Grandma Peaches react when you told them?" She asked.

"Exactly how you think they would. Dad seemed happy, but you know what Spencer's like, he keeps his emotions to himself sometimes. Mom was crying happy tears, as expected. I know she has been dying for a grandchild for so long. Grand Pa Miller is laid back, he just smiled, and chuckled. Grandma Peaches' reaction was incredible, you should have heard the way she screamed Tina. I suppose she's happy that she's alive to see all these huge milestones in my life. She saw me get married and now she'll be alive to see the birth of her first great-grandchild. I think you have some catching up to do Tina", Angela teased with a bright grin on her face.

Tina threw her head back in laughter and nodded her head, "Well there are somethings going on in my life that we have to talk about," she said.

Angela looked at her curiously and encouraged her to tell her everything.

Tina shook her head, "Not here, have lunch with me afterwards and I'll tell you everything,"

Once the yoga session was over, Angela and Tina left the building feeling thoroughly stretched out and relaxed as they walked through town together to find a nice and quiet lunch spot. Tina ordered herself a peach iced tea and Angela had gotten herself a refreshing glass of orange juice to sip on before digging into her salad. "So, then Tina, now that we're seated and eating, I think you ought to share that news you were so excited to share?" Angela asked. Tina took a sip of her drink and sat back with a coy smile on her face. "Well, I went grocery shopping sometime last week, and I had been looking for something to cook for my meal that night, unfortunately for myself and my rather small height, the thing I needed was all the way on the top shelf, I couldn't reach it for myself. That's when this tall, dark, and handsome gentleman approached me and pulled it down for me. Yes, I know it's rather weird to meet someone at the grocery store, but we started talking and he gave me his number",

Tina explained, wearing a huge grin the entire time. Angela squealed in excitement.

"Please tell me more, you must have gotten his number?"

"Yes, I did. We had dinner a couple of nights ago. I think he's so perfect Angela. He's studying to become a pharmacist, he also attends church every Sunday, so I know he's someone that Grandma Peaches would approve of", Tina said with a smile. Angela couldn't help but realize she was wearing the same kind of smile that she did, whenever she thought or talked about Richard. Co-incidentally, Angela had gotten a text from Richard that moment and her smile had dropped once she read over the message.

"What is it? Has Richard texted you?", Tina asked.

"Yes, he's asked me to come home. He said it's rather urgent", Angela told her. Tina nodded her head and agreed to drive Angela back to her home, once they quickly finished lunch with each other. Angela and Tina hugged each other goodbye, and she drove away as Angela walked to the front door of her home. She noticed a car was parked outside, but she knew it wasn't Richard's and she didn't recognize it as any of the neighbors' cars. The door to her house was already open and there were bags scattered everywhere, as well as a couple of suitcases left in the hallway.

"Richard! is everything all right?", Angela called out, looking around rather confused at all the suitcases in the room. Richard walked around the corner and greeted his wife with a very nervous smile, he walked towards her and pulled her into a hug.

"Hello my beautiful wife", He said.

"Hello to you too, I'm rather confused about that text you sent me, is everything ok Richard? And who do all these things belong to? It's making the hallway a mess", Angela asked. However, before Richard could respond. A grinning woman had walked around the corner and waved at the married couple. It was Richard's mother.

"There she is! the lovely woman who married my son and is now gifting me with a grandchild! It's so wonderful to see you again Angela", Richard's mother said, pulling Angela into a tight hug. Angela returned the hug kindly. Angela liked Richard's mother; she had helped them a lot when planning their wedding. However, his mother could sometimes be rather overbearing and liked to control a lot of things. Angela was even more anxious about why his mother would have turned up without announcing her arrival prior to her visit.

"It's great to see you also, I'm right in assuming these are all of your bags?", Angela asked.

"Yes darling! I had to make sure I had enough to last me a month", She said.

Angela's eyes widened with shock, she wasn't quite sure if she had heard her correctly, "I'm sorry, did you say a month?".

"Yes, myself and Richard's father thought we would come and stay with you for a month. I figured since Richard himself is going to be rather busy these days, you could use some help during this time in your pregnancy, there's the scans and check-ups you're going to have, I have to make sure that you're eating correctly and make sure you have everything set up for when the baby arrives", Richard's mom said, before excusing herself to the kitchen to cook them a meal for the night.

Angela turned to Richard with a tense smile, "Can I speak to you for a minute...in private", Angela said, leading them both to the privacy of the bedroom.

"Richard, your mother just said she's going to be here for a month", Angela said, the moment that the bedroom door had closed behind them.

"Yes, she did", Richard said nervously, pacing up and down the room.

"Don't get me wrong Richard, I like you very much. I don't think I can deal with your mother in our home for a month. I'm a grown woman and I like to think that I know how to look after myself. I can already tell that she's going to criticize me for everything I do", Angela complained with a small pout on her face.

"I could always tell her to leave"

"What, no! you can't do that. It's fine, it's only a month. In fact, she might not be that bad to handle", Angela said, trying to convince herself that perhaps a little extra help in the house might not be too bad. Richard nodded his head and pulled his wife into a hug.

"Exactly, she's just excited to be a grandmother. I promise my mother will behave." Richard's mother did not behave. Over the past couple weeks that Richard's parents had been living with them. His mother had been unbearable. It started first with Angela's kitchen, his mother had rearranged the whole kitchen overnight, so that she could find the cups and cutlery much easier. Angela only realized how much of a problem it was when she found pots and pans in her cup cupboard. His mother had also taken over Angela's garden had pulled out some of her favorite plants to plant her own fruit and vegetables. That upset Angela the most, as the garden was her most treasured area of the house. Angela was also unable to eat some of her favorite foods, or the food that she craved for due to his mother as she insisted that what she was eating was doing no good for the baby, and that she should try better at consuming her fruits and vegetables. Angela started to feel as though she had no control over what she did in her own home and pregnancy. She wanted to confront her mother-n- law but was too afraid of coming across as rude or disrespectful, so she allowed it to carry on and instead chose to call home and ask for her family's advice.

"She's just very excited Angela, give her a couple more days and I'm sure she will calm down", Angela's mother said.

"Women love babies, she's just trying her best and perhaps doing too much without realizing it, just be stern and respectful with her, I'm sure she will get the message", Spencer said.

"It can be difficult and at times stressful having your in-laws around your home. Remember at the end of the day it is your home and you have a right to be comfortable in your own space. Just remember to pray every night for the patience you need, my darling", Grandma Peaches advised.

Angela sighed. She had already been doing everything she had told her to do. She prayed every night, before the couple had gone to sleep. However, the next day, the same things would keep happening. Richard's father had been quiet and kept to himself the whole time that they had been there. Perhaps he could have a word with his wife and tell her not to be so overbearing.

Angela had asked Grandpa Miller to speak with Richard's Father about the situation and see if he could talk calmly with her, so she wouldn't be to upset.

"I put the kitchen back the way you had arranged it", Richard's mother Helen declared one night. Angela walked into the kitchen and found that everything was exactly the way she had organized it the day she had moved in. "I also replanted all those flowers you had, I know how much you loved them, and I feel bad for pulling them up without any second thought", She said, looking down at her feet with a guilty expression on her face. "Would you sit with me for a moment", she asked, sitting down on the couch, and patting the empty spot beside her.

"I'm trying to apologize Angela", she said, taking Angela's hand.

"My husband had a word with me the other night and I hadn't realized how invasive I had been until he told me everything I had been doing. I want you to know, that I know you can take care of yourself, you're a beautiful and mature woman. I suppose I got a little carried away", She said.

"A little?", Angela teased with a smile.

His mother chuckled, "Ok, I got massively carried away. Sometimes it can be hard to let go of your only child, I was so excited about bringing up another baby that I overlooked the fact that you are his wife and the mother and what you say goes. Could you forgive this old woman for her ways?".

"Yes of course, I will always forgive".

Richard came home that night, to find his wife and his mother sitting on the sofa together, laughing heartily at Richard's baby photos that his mother had brought along. It was embarrassing on his behalf, but at least the two most important women in his life we're getting along.

CHAPTER EIGHTEEN

THE SECRETARY

Angela led another Sunday school session. It was her favorite time of the day. More and more children from the church within the community had turned up to Angela's classes, as it appears more of the youth had been inspired. She had bonded with the children in the class and had a chance to learn all their personalities; she had a few class clowns, but she knew how to be firm enough to calm them down. Today she had decided that she would listen to the ideas that the children had shared with her a while ago about what they wanted to learn during Sunday School. The first things to come to her mind was to allow them to create and put on a play about their chosen bible story. The children had decided that they wanted to perform the story of the Good Samaritan at the church, to teach them about kindness. Angela thought it was a fantastic idea and so for the last couple of hours, she had been delegating parts to the children, creating a script for them to learn and a couple of songs that the children were enthusiastic about learning. Towards the end of the class, Angela noticed there seemed to be a commotion outside of the classroom. She held off her curiosity until she was finished with the children's class.

She made sure all the children had found their parents, before she quickly ran back towards where she had noticed the trouble, she had bumped into Martha on the way, who appeared to be rather stressed, with hair sticking up all over, "Is everything ok? I could hear all the noise and shouting outside my classroom but was unsure about what was going on?", She asked.

Martha huffed and shook her head, "You're probably best at going to see Richard, he's got his hands full, and I really have to head home now. I'll see you sometime next week, alright Angela?", Martha said, quickly hugging Angela before heading home.

Angela headed down towards the classrooms to find where the noise was coming from and was led towards the office where the church secretary usually worked, she could hear Richard inside mumbling to himself as things crashed around him inside the office. She stepped inside and was shocked by the utter mess that she witnessed. There were papers scattered all over the desk, on the floor and flying in the air as Richard was looking through them all. The phone was ringing repeatedly, but Richard was too busy to answer it and so it kept blaring throughout the office.

The church safe had also been left open. It was a disaster, and it didn't look good for the church.

"Richard, what on earth is going on in here?", She asked her Husband.

"Please don't worry about it Angela, as you can see, I have everything under control here", Richard said, almost falling backwards off his chair.

Angela snorted out in laughter at her husband, it was very clear that everything was in fact not under control in any type of way, "I think you must be mistaken my love, it's a complete and utter disaster in here the church safe shouldn't be open? What has happened? Have we been robbed? I surely hope not, the CCTV cameras would have notified us", Angela asked, starting to feel a little panicked. There was a lot of money that the church had raised, and it was all to go towards the church repairs.

"Don't worry, it's nothing of the sort. The money has been moved somewhere safe. The real problem is that we haven't had a church secretary for over a week", Richard explained.

"None at all? What happened to Sister Ruby? She hasn't come in all week?" She asked.

Richard shook his head.

"I'm going to give her a call. It's rather worrying that she hasn't turned up for a week. I'm going to make sure she is ok. Think you can handle things here for a moment?", Angela asked, although she couldn't help but cringe when she realized that she had to make the phone call a quick one, because Richard wasn't coping very well with the demand for work that had been left.

The phone rang a couple of times before a very quiet and weak voice answered the phone.

"Hello Angela, is that you?", Sister Ruby asked, before coughing a couple of times.

"Hello Sister Ruby, yes, it is me. I just heard from Richard that you haven't been in all week. I'm very worried about you and wanted to make sure that everything is alright at home?"

Sister Ruby sniffled through the phone, "I'm very sorry to make you both worry dear, but I'm afraid I've come down with a terrible illness, I have my children here looking after me, but if it gets any worse, I might have to go to the hospital. I'm not sure when I'll be able to return to work. I heard rumors of SARS virus developing in different countries. I am praying it hasn't reach the United States. I hope I haven't caused too much trouble", She coughed.

"No, of course not Sister Ruby, don't worry, me and Richard will be able to find someone to take over your duties until you feel well enough to return. Please make sure to look after yourself. I might come around later tonight and bring you a soup that my grandmother used to make for me when I was sick"

"That's very kind of you dear, I'll see you later"

"Bye", Angela hung up the phone and walked back to the office.

"I'm afraid that Sister Ruby isn't going to be returning anytime soon," She told him.

Angela and Richard agreed that they would try to balance the work between each other until they could find someone who had the time to take over the church secretarial duties. They would continue to do it themselves, however Richard was busy planning services and working his second job and Angela was busy with the Sunday School sessions and going through her pregnancy, therefore they needed extra help. During service, Richard and Angela looked around for people they could trust to take over the job. They approached Martha as their first choice, however Martha worked a full-time job and always had her grandchildren around her house and therefore didn't have the time to take over the church secretary job.

After service, Angela saw Holly and Cameron, she thought that perhaps she could ask Holly to take over the role. She trusted Holly to take care of things and be organized, therefore she walked over to the couple with the bright smile, "Hello you two, pleasure to see you as always, although I have an ulterior motive for coming over here and was hoping I could persuade you into helping out at the church," Angela told them.

Holly chuckles and nodded her head, "I'm always happy to help the church, what can I do for you Angela?"

"You see, our church secretary, Sister Ruby, had unfortunately fallen very ill. Richard and I had been trying to share the workload between us, but we're finding it hard to balance the other hectic things going on in our lives. We really wanted someone that we could both trust to take over the role of our church secretary, until Sister Ruby can return", Angela told her. "And you're both trusting me?" "Yes of course, if you were willing to take over the role, Richard and I would be so grateful for you"

"What kind of work am I expected to do?", Holly asked curiously.

"Most of the time, it's answering phone calls, many of our church members call in during the week, wanting to know what we're planning or wanting to speak with myself or Richard. There's also managing the church schedules that Richard will put in at the end of every week for the next. There's also filing and generating programs for services. Do you think this is something you could do?", She asked.

Holly looked at Cameron, before eagerly nodding her head, "Yes of course, I have work experience as a secretary and within the office. I'm sure my husband won't mind me being away for a few hours a day", Holly said. Angela sighed in relief and pulled Holly into a big hug.

"Thank you so much, you are saving my life", Angela said.

Holly agreed to stay behind after church so Angela could show her around and give her a place to start.

Things were back on track because of hiring Holly onboard to fill in as secretary. Angela had more time in the day to focus on her Sunday School sessions and work with the children on the play they were putting on for the church. She also had time to read the baby books she had bought in preparation for the baby. Richard was also much more relaxed now that he didn't have to work a third job and came home in the evenings looking less tense. Holly was wonderful at organizing things and the programs she created for services were perfect, it was almost better than what

Sister Ruby used to do. However, Angela wasn't seeing everything that was going on behind the scenes. There were a group of women in church that didn't like how close Holly had gotten with the church and the fact that she held a position, considering the past that Holly had.

Angela only realized something had been wrong, when she had walked past Holly's office one night and found her rubbing her temples, appearing thoroughly stressed. Angela knocked on the door to announce her presence, and Holly looked up at her with a forced smile.

"Hey, I was just getting something to drink, I noticed that you're looking a little stressed as I was passing by, is everything ok Holly? Is this work too much? we can always hire a second person to help you out in here?", Angela had offered, however Holly shook her head.

"No, everything is alright here. It's easy once you get the hang of it"

"Then what's wrong?"

Holly sighed and lowered her head, "It's a few women in the church. Sometimes they might call up and as soon as they hear my voice answering the call, they hang up. I can hear them whispering sometimes in service. I don't think they like me being here, like I don't belong in the church," Holly said.

Angela frowned. She didn't like the thought that there were members of the church that were pushing Holly aside. Especially since Holly had dedicated her like to Jesus Infront of everyone during Altar call. "That's terrible Holly. You do belong in the church; you are living as a Christian and have been a huge help here. Unfortunately, there a few older members who lack understanding and are judgmental. I think a service based on acceptance must be in order", Angela comfort her. Holly smiled and nodded her head.

"Thank you, Angela, don't worry about me. Get back to what you were doing, and I'll do some work here", Holly said, appearing more motivated after her talk with Angela.

Angela had told Richard about what people of the church were doing to Holly and he agreed that he ought to deliver service on forgiveness, acceptance, and judgement. Angela realized that the group of women that had been casting Holly aside, were the same members that didn't like the fact that Richard was going to be taking over from the Church's old pastor. At the end of service, Angela addressed the church and told them, "We as members of the church have a duty to look after one another. We do not exclude, we do not push aside, and we do not judge, remember; He that is without sin among you, let him first cast a stone, John 8:7." Angela wanted the women to know, that by judging Holly, they are not defining who she is, but defining themselves.

CHAPTER NINETEEN

TWINS

Working two jobs never became easier for him. Richard tried so hard to balance up the whole thing; but he had to strictly define his work hours and church hours, and he also had to dedicate some family time to his expectant wife. Sundays, Wednesdays, and Fridays, he dedicated to God; on Wednesdays he would work a half of a day just so he could meet up for bible study while on Friday, he worked from home so that he could take counseling. Whatever comes up when he was not around, Holly would bring it to the attention of Angela and if it was something she couldn't solve, Richard would take care of it when he comes back.

"My hospital appointment is on Tuesday; I would be having my first scan also." Angela informed Richard when he walked into their bedroom. He removed his wristwatch and placed it on his bed side table. He didn't say anything, but his eyes were wandering as though he was thinking. "You are not saying anything." She said.

"I am just trying to calculate my schedule for that day. It would be difficult to leave work babe, what time is the appointment, if it falls during my lunch hour, I might be able to risk It." he explained. He sat next to her on the bed and wrapped his arms around her shoulders.

She understood his point. He hadn't been working for long and the head of his department at the office understood the fact that Richard was a pastor and gave him some time for his ministry. Richard did not want to overstep or take advantage of his boss's kindness, so he took his job seriously whenever he was in the office and made sure he finished any outstanding work, or he took it home to finish up. for instance, he had to leave early on Wednesdays so he could conduct weekly activities (Bible study), and any job he couldn't finish, he would carry home and work on it after service or make sure he arrived to work extra early the next day to make up for it. Then most Thursdays, he stayed back late to finish up what he had to do in the office because he would be working from home the next day (He dedicated his Fridays to counseling and used his free time to work). "It's alright I know you will be busy, I just wanted to inform you to see if there would be any bit of hope." She said quietly.

"If you want, I could ask Tina to go with you." Richard told Angela.

"I'm not sure she will be free, the last time she came around, she said something about their record label organizing a talent hunt in our community back at home and it would really take up her time." Angela explained. She knew if she told Tina, she wouldn't hesitate to make herself available. But she would have to arrive that morning and leave immediately after the appointment which might be risky considering the distance from Alabama.

"My mother would be elated to go with you." Richard raised his brow. "That is of course if you want her to be there with you." Angela chuckled. "It is a perfect idea." Since Richard's mother apologized to her about how she had behaved when she first came, the two women had gotten along well. Helen took caution and allowed Angela to be the woman of her home. She assisted her with the garden and even chores around the house. She did not want her to over stress herself. She had enough on her plate already. Sometimes, they prepared dinner together and even shared recipes. "I will talk to her then." Richard told Angela and stood up from the bed. "I need to freshen up." he gave her a deep kiss on her lips before finally leaving for the bathroom. Angela prayed in her heart that it doesn't get worse than this. She knew that Richard might not be able to continue both ministry and work simultaneously it would wear him out. But he was adamant, he wanted to make sure that his family lacked nothing. In his words, "diapers and milk powder don't come cheap these days." he was the man of the house, and it is in his instinct to provide for them both. But in as much as he needs to provide, he also needs time for himself, to put in mental health in check, for her and for their unborn kids. The church also needs him, he cannot pour from an empty cup. When Richard came back into the bedroom, he laid next to Angela on their matrimonial bed, and they prayed together before they fell asleep.

Tuesday came, Richard was preparing for work. Angela came into the room to inform him that his breakfast was ready. Since he started his job with Apple, Angela took it upon herself to always prepare lunch for him to take to work. He had told her to stop stressing herself that he would take care of himself at work, but she didn't see it as a big deal, besides she barely prepared lunch every morning, most of the time, it was leftovers from the previous dinner especially when they invited guests over and she made one than on delicacy. She knew that if she didn't do it that way, Richard wouldn't mind staying the whole day and eat only when he gets home in the evening. It wasn't a good idea to starve himself of food when he wasn't fasting. "Babe, your breakfast is ready." She told him. He was struggling to get his tie knotted. "Let me help you with that." she advanced towards him and stopped in front of him. He places his hands on her waist and relaxed himself

"There you go." She tapped his shoulders.

"How did you learn how to knot a tie so easily?" he asked her smiling. "I haven't even learned it my whole life."

"I learned it from my dad. When I first came here, I noticed he didn't wear a tie often, there were times when he wanted to, but couldn't. One day, I asked him why and he said my mom use to help him out. That very day, I spent the whole day watching YouTube videos and practicing different types of ties. I never knew it would be of help to me with my husband." She explained to him.

"I see." He placed a feathery kiss on her lips. "I want to give you something." He let go of her waist and walked straight to the drawer and opened it. "Here, take this." He placed something into Angela's hand and covered it. Angela gasped. She couldn't believe it; he had handed her the keys to his sports car. "I thought we only use this for special occasions." She reminded him. "Why are you handing it to me?"

"Because my darling, you are special and there is no occasion more special than you." He looked into her eyes. "I may not always be available to take you wherever you want to go, but I cannot have you taking buses or spending extra cash on cabs with our unborn child when we have another car at home." Angela hugged him tightly. She loved him so much, he was everything she wanted in a man. They were two imperfect humans who had vowed to look beyond their imperfections and decided to make things work. Marriage was not a complete bed of roses, but they were ready to make sacrifices to make theirs work and be an exemplary couple to the church and community at large. "Thank you." She began to sob. "I love you so much, you are heaven sent. God sent you to me to show me how it feels to be loved and cared for in the right way. Thank you so much." For a few seconds, Angela's mind wandered into her past. She remembered how she felt she was late because all her friends were getting into relationships and getting married, but she chose to focus on God and her studies. How she got entangled in a mess with Charles. She was long gone! In that moment she was hugging Richard, she thanked God for not letting her go, she thanked God for finding her like he promised in the story of the lost sheep and the lost coin. Now, she was happily married to a man who loves God and loves her as God has instructed, she was a testimony and she knew that one day, she would share her story and she would inspire and be a blessing to a lot of young adults. Her mind went to Isaiah; the son of the pastor in her former church, he had been a friend indeed since whatever happened between them. Although, he did not make it for their wedding because he was out of the country.

"Stop crying babe, you deserve this and more." He used his thumb to wipe her tears. "Why are you being so emotional? He asked her laughing.

"I don't know," she blinked. "It's my hormones." She laughed. "Well, the hormones better make you smile more often, I hate seeing you cry." He held her hands. "I have to eat my breakfast now, or else I will be late." He told her as they both walked downstairs to the dining room making small talks. "What time is your appointment?" he asked her.

"11am." She answered.

"Have you told my mom?" he asked her. "So, she can get herself ready, and be on time."

"Soon to be Grandma Helen has been ready since six this morning." Richard burst into a fit of laughter. His mother was a drama queen, she was so excited about Angela's pregnancy as though she was the one carrying the baby herself. He couldn't wait for the drama to end as soon as Angela finally gives birth and Ashley moves in too.

"Good morning mom." Richard greeted his mom as he walked towards the dining. She was already having her breakfast.

"Good morning son." She answered. Richard got to where she was seated and gave her a peck on her cheek.

"I can see that you are ready for the day." Richard remarked.

"Yes son, I am so excited." She replied. Angela laughed. If Richard's mom could wear a shirt with a *"Go grandma"* print on it, Angela was sure she would not hesitate to grab the offer.

After Richard ate his breakfast, he grabbed his laptop bag and lunch pack and headed straight for the garage.

Angela and her mother in-law got to the hospital before eleven, when she got to the receptionist, she was asked to wait and would be called upon when it is her turn. At fifteen minutes past eleven o'clock, the nurse came to her and apologized for wasting her time because the patient before her is taking more time consulting with the doctor. "Its fine," Angela told the nurse "Just let me know when it is my turn." She told the nurse. When the patient came out, the doctor took a few minutes to freshen up and review Angela's file before she asked the nurse to invite her in. "Mrs. Richardson." The nurse called. "Yeah?" Angela answered. "You can go in now." Angela and her mother went into the office.

"Hello Doctor" Angela waved at her when she entered the office. "Good morning."

"Good morning Angel, how is your husband and the ministry?" she inquired. "Please take your seats" she offered the two women.

"My husband is doing well" Angela smiled "and the church is moving forward in God's marching order."

"That is good to hear." The doctor smiled.

"Meet my mother in-law, Mrs. Helen." Angela introduced the doctor to her mother in-law.

"Wow, ma you are looking so young. Who would have thought that you have given birth to a grown man as Pastor Richard?" she complimented Helen.

"God gives me the glow." Helen smiled as she replied to the doctor.

"God is good." The doctor answered.

Angela just sat down smiling, she liked how the two women were talking.

"You are here on behalf of your son I see." The doctor remarked, she was asking just to know if she could discuss sensitive issues in her presence.

"Yes Doctor" Angela replied to the doctor. "You see, my husband is at work. So, he couldn't make it here today, that is why he asked his mother to accompany me here. You are free to discuss anything in her presence, she is a mother to me too." Angela explained.

"Ok. Now that has been established, let's get down to business. How are you doing Angela?" the doctor asked her.

"I have been good, absolutely fine." She answered. The doctor nodded her head to urge her to continue speaking. "Aside from the morning sickness which you said its quite normal during the first trimester of most pregnancies, I really haven't noticed anything that would call for concern. I take my prenatal pills regularly, I take walks in the evening with my husband as an exercise, and I also eat fruits often. I do not stress myself about doing chores because my mother in-law assists me in whatever ways she can."

"Thank you, ma, for being of great help." The doctor thanked her.

"If I do not do it for her, who then would I do it for?" Helen replied smiling. She is appreciative of all the accolades that Angela had been showering on her since they walked into the doctor's office.

"I specifically warned her to stay away from anything stress and make sure she has enough time to rest because the last time she was in my office, her blood pressure was slightly above normal. Women with high blood pressure during pregnancy mostly have complications during delivery which could lead to us carrying out a caesarian section for them." She explained.

Now let me check your vital signs. She asked Angela to stand up from the visitor's chair and sit on the bed by the side of her office. The doctor carried her sphygmomanometer to where Angela was seated. "Your left arm." She requested and Angela stretched it forth for her. She wrapped the cuff around her arm and connected it to the monitor. When the results were out, she picked up Angela's file and wrote the results down. She checked her pulse and her temperature. "Why are you tensed?" the doctor asked Angela.

"I'm not." Angela answered with a smile.

"Your heart is beating very fast, and your pulse rate is high." The doctor told her, "You have to calm down, everything is fine, and there is no cause for alarm."

"Thanks doctor."

"Are you ready for your first scan?" the doctor asked her.

"Would it determine the sex of the baby?" Angela asked back.

The doctor laughed lightly. It is too early; we cannot be completely sure about the sex of the baby just yet because it wouldn't be clear as the baby is still developing.

"Let's go to the scan room." She said and gave Angela a bottle of water to drink. "It aids better visualization when your bladder is full." She explained.

Angela laid on the flat surface for scanning purposes in the scanning room, the ultrasound technician rubbed a jelly like substance on her stomach before using the ultrasound transducer on her. Helen stood next to Angela and held her hand throughout the whole process.

They went back to the doctor's office to await the result of the scan. The scan result was sent to the doctor's computer she displayed it on a bigger screen for them and explained the scan. "Congratulations Angela, you are having a set of twins." She announced.

For a few seconds, Angela could not process what the doctor had said to her. Helen had already stood up from the chair she was seated in to celebrate.

"Angela?" the doctor called.

"Doctor, what you said just now, please say it again."

"I said you are having a set of twins." She smiled. She understood the reaction, she had seen it too many times when she either announced to couples who were looking for the fruit of the womb that they were expecting or when she announced to women who were already pregnant that they were expecting twins.

"Jesus is so wonderful!" Was all that Angela was able to say. The news had overwhelmed her that she had to take her time to rest in the waiting room before driving her and her mother-in-law back home.

CHAPTER 20

SURPRISES

Angela begged her mother in-law to keep the news to herself until Richard gets back home, she wanted to surprise Richard with the news herself. She decided to make Richard's favorite meal for dinner, chicken, and roasted vegetables. She wanted to inform Richard first before telling the rest of her family, she knew that if she told them now, they might call Richard to congratulate him too. During Richard's lunch hour at work, he picked up his phone to call Angela, to ask her how her appointment with the doctor went, "Hello love, how are you?" he asked her.

"I am doing great, how is work?" she asked him.

"So far so good." He answered,

Angela sighed.

"How was your appointment today?" he asked.

"Fine, it was fine." She answered shortly.

Richard was expecting her to give him a breakdown of how the entire meeting played out but the only thing she said was fine. "How is your blood pressure?" he asked her.

"The doctor said it's normal and that I have nothing to be scared of." She answered him, she was fighting so hard not to reveal the good news to him over the phone.

"Did she still carry out the scan?"

"Babe, I need to go now, your mom needs my attention, I will see you when you get back home, love you." She rushed off the phone. She blew kisses and ended the call. "He was being too inquisitive she said to herself."

She walked to the kitchen to assist her mother in-law in slicing the vegetables.

"I have it covered." She told Angela, "Just start grilling the chicken."

Angela walked to the table where she had kept the marinated chicken, took the cooking brush to rub oil on it before putting it in the grilling machine. Helen's phone rang.

"It's Richard." She told Angela as she answered the call. "Hello son" she answered, "How are you?"

"I am fine mom. How was the appointment today?" he asked his mom.

"Hello?" she pretended as if she didn't hear what he had said. "I will call you back, I am in the kitchen. Angela and I are preparing dinner, it's your favorite." She hung up immediately.

The two women locked eyes and burst into a fit of laughter.

"Thank you, Angela," Helen finally said when she regained herself from the laughter.

"What did I do?" she asked Helen.

"For everything; being the best daughter in-law there is to be, being a perfect wife for my son and now, you are about to bless this family with two beautiful kids need I say more?" A tear slipped from her eyes.

Angela walked up to her and embraced her. "Thank you." When Richard came home from work, Angela welcomed him as usual and helped him with his bag.

"Dinner is ready, but you have to freshen up first." She placed a quick kiss on his lips then he made his way to their bedroom while she took his back to the study room.

The family sat down at the table and said their prayers before they began to dig into their food. "Do you like the food baby?" Angela asked Richard.

"I love it!" he answered her smiling. She could tell from the way he devoured the meal leaving no bone unskinned.

"Thank you, your mom assisted me in preparing it." Angela remarked. She did not want to take all the glory for the beautifully prepared meal. Besides Helen was a great help, she gave her some new tips in preparing it and Angela liked the outcome.

"Oh, that's great, thanks mom." Richard thanked his mother.

"You are welcome son."

The table was quiet for a while then Richard asked; "Did you still carry out the scan today?" he directed to Angela.

"Yes, I did." She answered enthusiastically.

"What did it say?" he asked. He was eager to know, he did not fail to notice how Angela and his mom had avoided his question earlier in the day.

"Hold on, let me get the result." She flashed her perfect set of while teeth and stood up from the chair. She came back in a flash and handed the envelope to Richard. He took it and opened it. Before it could read the result, Angela broke the news herself. "We are having twins!" she shouted.

Richard's eyes quickly scanned through the result and saw it, he could not believe his eyes. This is indeed a great surprise. He stood up from his chair and hugged

Angela tightly. He rained kisses on her face. "Thank you, Jesus!" He kept on saying. "Have you told Grandma Peaches and your mom yet?" he asked.

"Not yet, I wanted you to know first." She explained.

"What are we waiting for? Let's put a call across to them right away." He took his phone and dialed spencer's number, he picked up on the second ring.

After exchanging pleasantries, Richard broke the news to him. It happened while everyone was in the sitting room watching a movie together, "Everyone, Angela is having twins." He announced. Grandma Peaches quickly walked over to him and took the phone, she put it on speaker and spoke to her. She blessed the name of the lord for smiling upon her grandchild. Congratulations were in order, grandpa miller congratulated her and Ashley too. Ashley offered to move in with Angela to help her so she wouldn't stress herself too much, but Angela declined saying Helen was already with her and has been very helpful. Ashley should save all her strength for when the babies are born.

Angela asked about Tina, but she was told that Tina was working late because of the talent hunt her record label was organizing, so she decided to call her and break the news to her.

"Hey girl!" Tina saluted Angela.

"I heard you were working late." Angela replied.

"Yeah, I told you about the talent hunt, right? You will not believe the voices I heard. There are a lot of people to be discovered in the small town." Tina replied to her.

"Wow."

"Yeah, the record label has promised a cash prize and a recording contract with the winners though."

"That's great." Angela would have probably auditioned if she was still in Alabama. She remembered how she use to lead songs for St. John's Baptist church.

"Yeah, it's a way of giving back to the society. What's up?" Tina asked. She knew her cousin didn't call her just because of the talent hunt program the record label she was working for organized.

"I went for my first ultrasound today." Angela announced.

"I know it is going to be a girl!" Tina shouted.

Angela laughed. "It is too early to determine the sex of the babies Tina."

"Babies?" Tina asked confused. She was unsure and wanted clarification.

"Yes dear, babies! I am carrying twins." She announced.

Tina let out a shriek. "Congratulations!"

"Thank you." Angela replied.

"Well, I have news for you too." Tina told Angela. Her voice became calm and steady.

"Shoot." Angela told her.

"I said yes to him, I am finally in a relationship with Eric." She announced.

Eric was the guy she had told Angela that she met at the supermarket,

"I am so happy for you darling, as long as he has the fear of God and he treats you well, he is welcomed. I cannot wait to meet him." Angela grinned from ear to ear.

"Thank you, Angela. I need to go now; the day will soon be over."

"Alright, good night." Angela wished her and ended the call.

Everyone was happy about the good news of the babies that Angela was carrying.

She went to the study room to meet Richard but found out that he was on a call with holly. She was briefing him about all that had happened at church and the calls and appointment he has. Holly was doing a good job being Richard's secretary, even if ruby recovers and comes back to the job, Angela would ask holly to stay back and work together with ruby to make the job easier for them.

That evening, Angela got a call from an old friend, Isaiah. "Oh Isaiah, what a pleasant surprise." She said to him as she tried to adjust her web cam. "Good evening, Angela, it has been a while." He smiled. It has been a while indeed, Angela thought to herself. She hadn't seen Isaiah since she left home, they had only communicated through calls, either video or voice call. "Look at you" she smiled. "You are back in town?" she asked him.

"Yeah, I came back a week ago." He replied to her. It seemed like someone called out to him in his house because he replied, "I'm on a call!" Angela just smiled at the camera. "So, this is the first time I am seeing your face since you got married," he laughed "I am sorry I couldn't make it." He had apologized repeatedly on the phone.

"I' heard you Isaiah, I understand you were not able to make it. I do not hold any grudge against you, however, I am still expecting my wedding gift" she teased.

Isaiah laughed. "Well, if that's what it would take to earn your forgiveness then expect something soon."

"Oh wow, I know you to be a man of your word. Thank you." Angela replied to him. Isaiah was someone who kept his word, she remembers how he had previously helped her cover her shame. He promised her he wouldn't tell anyone, and he never did until she spoke about it herself.

"I spoke to grandma peaches on Sunday, she was so excited to see me, she kept on talking about you. She said you were expecting, congratulations." He congratulated her. He was genuinely happy that

Angela had found happiness in the midst of the storm that had troubled her life.

"Yeah," she smiled shyly "I just found out that I am expecting twins." She broke the news to him. He deserved to know.

"Whoa! Glory! God is awesome." He exclaimed.

"God is indeed awesome." She smiled.

"You must definitely come to Atlanta once I give birth."

"My husband and I would be delighted to see you." She told him. Angela had told Richard everything about her past, she left no stones unturned. Richard and Isaiah exchange pleasantries from time to time during phone calls with Angela.

"Then maybe afterwards you guys would visit Alabama for my wedding." He broke the news.

"Wait, what?" she was surprised.

"You heard me Angela, I'm getting married." He smiled. "You will meet her soon."

Angela was genuinely happy for Isaiah; she knew how much he loved her and how greatly she had hurt him. She prayed for him every time he crossed her mind for God to give him his perfect fit just as he had given to her.

"I am so happy for you. I would definitely come to Alabama." She gave a thumbs up. Just then, Richard walked into their bedroom. "My husband is here." She informed Isaiah. "Babe, Isaiah is getting married soon." She told Richard.

"Oh, that's good news." Richard walked up to where Angela was seated and greeted Isaiah. They exchanged pleasantries.

"I need to go now, good night." Angela told Isaiah.

"Good night." Then he ended the video chat.

Angela put the laptop down and pulled her husband in for a tight hug. "Hugs help to relieve stress." She smiled.

"Thanks."

"How are the affairs of the church?" she asked him.

"God has everything under control and holly is doing a good Job." He answered her.

"I spoke to sister ruby earlier today; she is getting better. She might resume next week with all things being equal." She told him. She knew Richard was too busy to check up on her, so she calls on behalf of him

and never forgets to add "Richard sends his regards."

CHAPTER 21

BABY SHOPPING

Richard closed from work early on Wednesday to be able to prepare for bible study. He had given Angela the key to his other car, so he did not have to bother driving home to pick her and his mother up before driving to church. Angela helped him select the clothes he would wear during the service she put them in his car that morning, so all he had to do was change in his church office. Shortly after Richard got to church, Angela and his mother arrived. The service went smoothly, Richard talked about life after accepting Jesus. He made the church to understand that God loves us all and Jesus came to die for the sinners that was why in the parable of the lost sheep, Jesus left the ninety-nine and went after the one that was lost. He had ninety-nine, why did he care so much about that one? Because the lost one was a sinner and Jesus cares for sinners. He read the book of Isaiah chapter 1 verse 18 which talked about cleansing us of our sin once we accept him. It said, "Though your sins are like scarlet, they shall be as white as snow; though they are red as crimson, they shall be like wool." He told the church that God doesn't look at us by our sins by the time we have accepted him. We have become new creations and old things are passed away. No matter the sin we have committed, it is left for God to judge and not we as humans. He also read the book of romans 8 verse 1 which says therefore, there is now no condemnation for those who are in Christ Jesus. The fact that everyone's private life is not in the open does not mean that we are all without cockroaches in our cabinets. He urged the church to love one another sincerely with their whole hearts because the church is not a place for judgment but a place for healing, to connect and feel God's presence. "Different people have different problems bothering them, they come to feel whole again, but because some of us who think we are without sin judge them or seclude them, and they end up going home even worse than they had come." Richard instructed them to mingle with people after service, meet someone you haven't talked to before and give them a friendly hug. After the message, Holly and Cameron felt even more connected to God, for the first time, they felt like they genuinely belonged. The set of elders who were against Holly handling the position of the secretary in church came to her and hugged her one after the other. Everyone made new friends. It was an awesome service.

"You did great today in church." Angela complimented her husband. Any time Richard stood on that pulpit to share God's word, she knew that God was using him because he wasn't sharing words of his own but the words that God had put in his mouth to share. She thanked God in her mind for giving her a man like Richard, a man who would allow God to use him. "All the glory goes to God. That topic has been brooding in my heart to share." Richard told her.

"It is a good thing you listened to the Holy Spirit because I believe it is him who had planted the topic for you. The church was so lively after service, even holly came to me and said for the first time since she and Cameron took the bold decision to give their lives to Christ, she felt fully accepted in Ambassadors of Christ Youth Ministry Church."

"That is great news." Richard smiled. He was happy that God had used him to make an impact in their lives.

He knew that there were many other people who felt left out, not really because they were chastised for their sins but because they had not been able to form a good relationship with other members of the church, so the moment the service was over, they picked up their bags and bibles and headed for the door of the church until the next service time.

Richard and Angela chatted a little more before they went to bed.

The next morning, Angela stood in front of the vanity mirror in her matrimonial room. She raised her top slightly to examine her baby bump; her tummy was no longer flat, and the bump was becoming more visible. She must start wearing freer clothes she said to herself. She used her left had to raise her top and her right hand to rub her belly gently. It was itching her a little, but she had been warned by Helen not to because scratching will cause stretch marks on her tummy after giving birth and she did not want that. Richard came out of the bathroom with a towel around his waist and hugged her from behind.

"Oh, please stop." Angela complained.

"Can't I hug my wife?" he asked raising one of his brows jokingly.

"Of course, you can, but not with your wet body. Clean up first at least." She told him and let her top drop. Richard let go of her and began to clean the water off his wet body.

"You are looking even more beautiful by the day." Richard complimented her. He looked at her with so much admiration. Even though she was pregnant, she still maintained beauty.

"You mean I am looking even fatter by the day." Angela remarked. She knew she had added a few pounds which was quite normal because of the children she was carrying but she was worried. Will she go back to her beautiful before-pregnancy body size, or will she retain this size or drop just a few pounds? Will her husband still find her attractive? Her unvoiced fears were beginning to creep in.

"This is just a pregnancy feature, with the right diet and exercise, you would get your body back after you give birth. You look beautiful dear, even with your full cheeks. You are beautiful smart and hardworking." He comforted her.

"Thank you." She smiled shyly. Richard knew how to use words. With just three sentences, he had vanished all her fears.

When Richard was done cleaning his body, he proceeded to put on his clothes. Helen had told Angela to sit back and rest she would handle breakfast and Richard's lunch by herself. Even when Angela protested and offered to assist, Helen refused so she went back to the bedroom.

"Babe." Richard called Angela's attention.

"Yeah?" she replied then sat on the bed.

"You are fourteen weeks gone already and we need to start preparing for our babies fully, we do not have enough time on our hands. We need to start buying the babies' things and preparing their room."

Angela nodded her head in agreement. "I have saved up some money and we could start buying the most important things." He concluded. "I have some savings too. I will add them up. Thank you for being the helpmate of this family." Richard replied by giving her a kiss on her lips.

"I will check some children's room designs online and show them to you when you get back home in the evening. Then we can call the painter to do justice to their room. As for the buying of the things, I would want Tina to be free first before embarking on such quest." She told Richard. Even without further explanation, Richard already knew the reason why Angela would want Tina to go with her for shopping. His mother can be overbearing sometimes and would not let her make some of her decisions. But Tina was strong headed and fierce and would stand up to Helen for Angela. Angela helped him knot his tie and they both headed to the dining room for breakfast.

When Richard left the house, Angela called Tina to ask her when she would be free to go shopping with her and her mother-in-law. Tina felt delighted that Angela wanted her to be there, she picked the following weekend, by then they would have rounded up the talent show, and she would have more time on her hands. When they had finished talking, Angela prepared herself for church, she had rehearsals with the children at church for their drama presentation the following Sunday. They were going to illustrate the story of the Good Samaritan. It was a good follow up to the sermon that Richard had taught the previous day.

The following weekend, Tina came to Atlanta as promised and she went with Angela and Helen to shop for baby things. Angela was so excited to be shopping for her babies. These items would make her feel more connected to her unborn twins, it would become clearer in her eyes that she was expecting and that she was going to be a mother to two beautiful kids. She had the option of shopping online but decided to go by herself to a physical store so she could see what she was getting and make choices between different products, sizes, and prices. The amount of time it would take for delivery from ordering online would make her have anxiety. Angela was able to buy baby cribs, double cots, linens and blankets, napkins, changing mats and diapers, a baby tub together with towels, soap, shampoo, oil, and a set of baby combs. She also got feeding bottles, cups and spoons and a few toys and some first wears for babies. She refrained from buying too many clothes because she did not know the sex of the babies yet. The money that Richard had given her took her a long way, but Tina surprised her by transferring cash to Angela at the mother care shop. "You do not have to." Angela refused.

"Well, there isn't much you can do, the money is already in your account and besides, I want to do it for you, for my god children. Take it as my first gift to them." Tina convinced Angela. Drops of tears escaped Angela's eyes. She hugged Tina at the shop.

The only time Helen wanted to make a fuss was when she insisted Angela buy a baby crib instead of a cot. Angela tried to convince her that the cot was better because of longevity, thankfully, Tina sent her some money to contribute to the shopping and she was able to get the cribs. When they got back to the house, Angela couldn't wait for Richard to get home, so she quickly made a short video of the items they had got and sent it to him. Richard was joyful, it just dawned on him he was going to be a father to two beautiful babies. His joy was short-lived when the head of his department at his office at work called him and wanted to see him.

Angela and Tina surfed through the net looking for suitable designs for the baby's room. "I want something simple, yet so elegant." She told Tina.

"It must be unique." Tina commented.

"Yes. I know it's a children's room, but I do not want those flashy colors, I want something neutral. I do not know how to explain it, but when I see it, I will identify it." Angela told Tina with a smile.

"I have an idea!" Tina blurted out. "What you want is unique which means rare. We might never get it here," she told Tina pointing to the web page on the tablet she was holding. "We need to find the right places."

"Where is the right place?" Angela asked Tina.

"Our minds, we are intelligent women. We have seen tons of samples online. Let us create our unique design and bring an interior decorator to bring it to life."

Angela smiled at Tina's idea. She loved it.

Angela quickly got a piece of paper and a pen, and the two women began to strategize.

CHAPTER 22

WHEN THINGS CHANGE

Richard looked upset when he arrived home that evening. He went straight to his study room and locked himself in there for hours. Angela could sense that something was not right. She went to him asking him, "My love." She called calmly. Richard's tie was loose around his neck and his long white sleeve was rolled to his arm's length. The room was cool, but beads of sweat had formed around his forehead. He sat down looking into space. "Babe." She called again. This time her eyes were teary. She had become emotional, "You are scaring me, tell me what's wrong. I have never seen you like this before."

Richard pulled her closer to him and made her sit on his lap as he wrapped his arms around Angela's body. "We will figure it all out." He spoke softly into her ears. Thousands of scenarios had flashed before her eyes. "You are scaring me." She replied. This time the tears that had been gathering around her eyes had finally fallen. "I got fired today." He broke the news softly. He felt Angela's body stiffen around his hand.

"What happened?" she asked. She felt sorry for her husband. He needed the job so badly just so he could make them comfortable. His instinct as a man to provide has been bruised. "I was in the office today when someone called me and said the head of my department wanted to see me. When I got there, he engaged me in a conversation totally unrelated just to lighten the mood then suddenly, he became serious and broke the news to me. In these were his words, he said; *I know that you are a pastor and a family man, the church is probably more important to you than this job even though it is obvious that you are putting in your best. This is a profitable organization, and we are profit minded. We are not yielding the result we expected of you Richard and so with careful thoughts and deliberation we have to let you go.* He did not even give me a chance to prove myself or even a few weeks probation period." He broke down in tears and began to sob on his wife's shoulder. "I'm sorry babe. Things would get better, I promise. We will sit together and pray for a better job. We are children of God and we have served him diligently; God cannot leave us hanging." She removed one of her hands from his wrap and began to pat his shoulders. Angela was very sure that God would not leave them hanging. The couple sat still for a while in silence then Angela broke into a worship song. Richard joined in and they both praised God together.

Richard did not eat dinner that night, he had asked Angela to wrap it and put it in the freezer, so she could microwave it the next morning.

In the morning, Richard woke up and prepared for church. It was a Saturday morning, he had informed Holly that he would be available for the whole day for prayers and counseling. He left even before Angela could microwave his food. She knew that he was still upset about what had happened the previous day, and he didn't have any appetite to eat but he just had to eat something for strength. He was not allowed to take out his anger and frustration on his meals, she hated the fact that he was rejecting her food.

She had her final rehearsals with the children in church that same day, so she dressed up in a *long* gown and carried her bag when Helen stopped her.

"Can I talk to you for a moment?" she asked.

"Yeah, of course." Angela dropped her bag on the sofa and sat on the edge of the chair.

"Is everything ok with Richard?" she asked. "With the two of you?" she was concerned. It was obvious that something was wrong with the way Richard was acting but Angela felt like it wasn't in her place to tell Helen what had happened. Helen was Richard's mother and if anyone was going to tell her that Richard had been laid off work between the two of them, it should be Richard.

"Hmm..." Angela heaved a sigh. "We are fine ma. But if there is any cause for concern, I think Richard will let you know by himself." She gave a dry smile.

"Alright, thank you Angela."

"You are welcome mom." Angela picked up her bag and headed for the garage.

A few months after Richard got laid off work, the couple coped well. Richard continued in his quest to search for a new job while Angela occasionally took on editorial and proofreading jobs and worked from home just to support the family. It wasn't easy for them because Angela was pregnant, and her mother in-law was in the house. Richard had once asked Angela if he should ask his mother to leave. Angela, forbid it saying, she has stayed too long already, why ask her to leave when her due date is approaching, and she has been helpful around the house. Church members were also helpful, they appreciated the fact that Richard led the church with the fear of God, few of the elders knew about his financial situation and were in awe of him because despite what he was going through, he was transparent with church finances. Sister Martha organized a meeting behind Richard and Angela with some of the elders, in conclusion they decided that Richard should be paid a monthly salary. They knew it would not solve their financial issues because it was a small amount, but it would at least go a long way. When Angela and Richard were called upon to hear the news, they couldn't believe their ears. They were shocked that the church cared for them in such manner. Week in and week out, members of the church would come around with gifts for Angela and the babies, some would go grocery shopping on behalf of the family and bring it to them. Cameron and Holly weren't left out, they tried to give support in whatever way they could.

One night, Angela got a call from her mother, Ashley.

"Hello Angela!" she sounded worried.

"Mom, what's wrong." She sat up on the bed, all her body had become alert.

Richard sat up too, "What's wrong?" he asked too.

"Your grandmother had a sudden heart attack!" Ashley blurted out. Her voice was croaked, she had been crying.

"What happened, is she fine now, what is the doctor saying?" were the series of questions Angela asked her mother on the phone.

"She is on oxygen and the doctors haven't said anything. Everyone is here, Grandpa Miller, your father and Tina. Pastor Brown is also here to pray for her, but the doctors haven't let anyone in yet." She explained.

Angela's eyes had swollen with tears. "I will come in the morning." Angela told her mother.

"No, you are not going anywhere." Richard cut her off.

"No Angela, I am not asking you to come, I just want to update you on what is happening, you cannot travel such distance in your condition." Ashley told Angela, she had even heard Richard's objection over the phone, and she was in support.

"Grandma Peaches is in the hospital on life support, and you are asking me not to come? It is Grandma Peaches we are talking about, she has to recover, and she hasn't met her great grandchildren yet..."

"Is that why you want to risk their lives?" he questioned her. "Are you the one going to heal her? Your mother just said her pastor is there and besides God is omnipresent, if you pray here, she can receive her healing over there."

Angela was quiet. It was obvious she had not thought about it thoroughly.

"There are many reasons you should not even go to Alabama, but you are not thinking. We are not even financially buoyant for that; we are only trying to take life one day at a time." Richard explained to her. Angela kept quiet. Richard saw that she was adamant, stood up from the bed and stormed out of the room.

Angela thought about everything Richard had told her, she had made her decision in the spur of the moment, and she was sorry. She stood up from the bed by supporting herself with her hands on the bed, her baby bump had grown bigger. She found him in the study room, he was reading a book.

"Knock, knock." She said as she stood in front of the room leaning on the door frame.

"Come in." he answered without looking up. She walked into the room with her hands on her waist as a form of support, her stomach going before her. She walked to where he was seated and stood in front of him. "I'm sorry." She said. Richard did not answer her, nor did he look up. "I did not think it through, you are right." Richard closed the book he was reading and looked up at her. "Come here." He wanted to hug her, but her protruding stomach obstructed him, they both burst into a fit of laughter. He stood up and hugged her from the back.

"I love you so much Angela Richardson." He professed to her.

"I love you too Pastor Richard Richardson. "Wow! What a tongue twister Angela said as she laughed.

CHAPTER 23

NEW LIFE

One fateful afternoon, Richard was in church supervising an ongoing project; the church had donated for the expansion of the children's wing. Angela's impact in the children's Sunday school had greatly influence more parents to send their children to church. Some parents who weren't even members of Ambassadors of Christ Youth Ministry started sending their children to Angela's Sunday school class, it became massive during the summer break. Angela got some volunteers from church including Sister Martha, Ruby, and Holly to teach the children. They learned stories about the bible, Angela taught them about the famous PANTS rule, known as the underwear rule in Europe for sexual abuse. It teaches children wear they should not be touch using pants and the underwear rule. She also educated the males among them on what it met to give consent. Angela learned this while she was in college. Martha, Ruby, and Holly Continued to teach the same things Angela taught the children in her absence. The women gave the youth a clear message about sexual abuse and its evilness. The lady who oversaw the after-service bake sale came around to teach them how to make cupcakes and cookies while a fashion designer came to teach them how to make hats and hair pieces. The children ended the summer classes with lots of knowledge. Richard's phone rang, when he looked at it, it was his mother who was calling. He quickly swiped the screen of his phone to take her call.

"Good afternoon mom." Richard greeted her.

"Angela is in labor!" she exclaimed over the phone. Richard could hear groans from the background. "Calm down honey, I will get the car ready." Helen soothed Angela. "I want you to bring the car to the front of the house; it will be easier for her to get in." she explained. Angela shrieked. "The babies are coming!" Angela shouted!

"Mom are you sure you can handle this?" he asked her worried. "Just wait for me, I'm coming to the house."

"Just meet us at the hospital, before you get here it might be too late, one of their heads would be out already." She laughed lightly.

"It is only my mother who can make jokes of such a situation." He said to himself.

When the call ended, he asked someone to call a particular elder inside the church. Richard explained to him that Angela was in labor and he needed to be with her, that the elder should stay in his place to supervise the church project. On his way to the hospital, he called Ashley to inform her about Angela's condition.

When Richard got to the hospital, he saw his mother standing outside the labor room. "Any news?" he asked her.

"Nothing yet, since they took her in, nurses have been entering and coming out, no one is saying anything." She sounds worried.

A nurse came out of the room and walked down to the corner where Richard and his mom Helen were pacing up and down, "Good afternoon, are you here for Mrs. Angela?"

"Yes" they both answered in unison.

"She is asking for her husband." The nurse informed them.

"I'm the one" Richard identified himself.

"Come with me, I will provide you with the necessary protection." Richard followed her immediately.

The labor room felt uncomfortable for Richard when he first got the room. He saw Angela lying on the delivery bed, she was naked but covered with a small cloth on her lower body, her legs were spread far apart. The doctors and nurses are all dressed in gowns, wearing masks and gloves.

"Sir, could you please stand over there." One of the nurses directed him to stand close to Angela.

"Your wife is getting weak, if she doesn't push now, she will have to have a caesarian section!" the doctor stated "She wanted you to be here while she makes her final attempt. We cannot risk both the life of the mother and the babies."

Richard nods his head in understanding. He leans close to Angela's ears and whispers to her, "Baby, you are about to become a mother to our beautiful children, you cannot afford to be weak right now, the race is not given to the swift, nor the battle to the strong, I ask for God's strength to come upon you right now." He proclaimed.

"Amen!" Angela shouted! "Give me your hand" she ordered Richard, He did as he was told.

"Ok guys, let's try again." The doctor called. "Alright Angela, take a deep breath, when I say push, you try your best to push your babies out." She told Angela.

"Ok." Angela answered. Beads of thick sweat had gathered around her forehead.

When the doctor made the call, Angela gave her all, she pushed with all her might and the first baby came out with a sharp cry.

"Baby number one is out; we go again for baby number two." The doctor told Angela. She was still holding Richard's hand tightly while he was busy praying silently. The sight of his wife in the labor room was one he could never forget; he was tensed but had to compose himself as a man. He told himself women deserve to be respected, especially mothers because bringing a child into the world was not an easy job to do.

"Baby number one is a girl, time of birth 3:16pm." A nurse announced. Richards's heart was full of joy, he could not wait to hold his baby girl. The doctor carried out the same process and at 3:28, baby number two came out. "Baby number two is a boy; time of birth is 3:28pm." The nurse announced again. The two babies were brought to Angela to hold them in her arms for a few seconds then they were carried away to be cleaned up. Angela had lost all strength in her, she relaxed completely on the bed feeling weak. Richard tried to clean some of the sweat off her forehead with his thumb. "Racheal and Richard Jr." She said softly.

"Racheal and Richard Jr" Richard repeated after her in confirmation.

"Sir, you will have to excuse us now, we need to clean her up."

Richard came out of the labor room and informed his mother, "It's a boy and a girl!" he announced.

Helen shouted for joy and gave Glory to God, she was elated.

Richard quickly put a call through to Ashley to inform her. Ashley told Richard that she would leave for Atlanta first thing in the morning, she just wanted the person who would help her care for Grandma Peaches to arrive first.

"Grandma Peaches, can you hear the good news? You are now a great grandmother." Ashley said to her mother. Grandma Peaches had not been able to fully recover after the sudden heart attack she had so from time to time, she was taken to the hospital for monitoring and treatment.

Richard also called Tina to inform her about Angela, she arrived in Atlanta on that same day, and she said she couldn't wait to see her godchildren

The next month felt like hell for Angela, their financial situation had gotten worse, Richard had to put his car up for sale but he hadn't seen a buyer yet. The couple were not happy, but they did not show it to the world. The two grandmothers who were living in the house could only suspect but could not get the hang of the whole situation. Angela was not eating well and yet she was breast feeding not just one but two babies who wanted to suck her milk dry. The only person who she could confide in about her situation was not even her best friend Michelle but her cousin and sister, Tina. Tina played her part by sending money to Angela occasionally even if Angela was not too comfortable with it. "Hey, you would do even more for me if I was in your position." Tina told Angela and she meant it, "Besides I am just doing my part as I have become an aunt and a god mother." She added to lighten up the mood. "I know God called Richard and he has been faithful to his work in the house of God, you are too. This is only a phase; God is about to launch you into greater miracles." Tina prophesied and Angela replied by saying "Amen."

Richard continued to apply for remote jobs because that would be the only kind of job that would give him the luxury of running the church without fearing getting laid off. He believed and had the conviction that his life was not meant to continue this way, he needed to be the man he should be to his family, a provider, and a leader. Ashley called home from time to time to check on her mother and was told that Grandma Peaches had greatly improved and would be coming to visit Angela and her twins with Pastor Brown in his private jet.

When Pastor Brown came, Angela and Richard were able to be open to him about their condition and he encouraged them, he told them that the devil attacks Christians especially church leaders to make them feel like their service for God is a waste. He urged them to pray fervently and that everything would turn out well, he was positive, in fact, he saw it happening soon.

Grandma Peaches was so happy to see her great grandchildren. She thanked God for keeping her alive till that day. Unfortunately for grandma peaches, she had to leave with Pastor Brown that same day, she had injections to take the next morning. "Grandma Peaches, you have to get better so that you can come back and spend a whole month with your great grandchildren." Angela comforted her.

"I will be back." She hugged Angela before she left with Pastor Brown. Grandma Peaches did not go back, she died exactly a month after she visited her great grandchildren. It was sad news for everyone. Grandma Peaches was a strict Christian who dedicated her life trying to instill good values into her grandchildren and young adults of the church, she was loved and will be greatly missed. Angela of course took the news hard. She couldn't sleep or eat. Life as she knew it would never be the same. She had lost her everything, she thought to herself. She could hear Grandma Peaches saying, "Child God is your everything." not me. Lean on him. All she could do was cry and cry. She knew Tina, her mom Ashley, and Grandpa Miller was hurting too. Angela just could not bring herself to talk to anyone. She wondered how Ashley got the strength to help her care for the babies. Her dad Spencer rushed over to comfort everyone, especially Ashley. She was still his wife and he loved her with all his heart. It had been years since he had touched her. As soon as he knocked on the door she fell into his arms and belted out a loud groan of a cry straight from the pit of her belly. He could smell the sweet smell of cherry blossom perfume as he held her close. They stood in the door with the door wide open with Spencer's backed propped up against the door hinges. Ashley sobbed and sobbed, and yell for her mom. Richard her the noise and ran to the doorway and grabbed Spencer's shoulder and pulled them inside while guiding them to the couch. Ashley still had a hold of spencer. He kisses her on her cheek and whispered baby I am here and I'm not going nowhere.

Just let me be here for you, I love you his eyes fill with tears. Ashley yells oh God Oh God! Angela hears the noise and grabs her covers and pulls them over her head. "This is a Dream; THIS IS A DREAM!"

"HELP ME LORD!" She yells. Not realizing she was making outbursts. Richard heard her and came running. Baby, Baby, I am here. God will heal your broken heart. Richard, I don't need a preacher right now! "If you are going to be here just be quiet."

"Ok, baby what do you need?" Richard kissed her softly.

"My grandmother! My sweet Grandma Peaches." Why now, now WHY!"

"God's timing." Richard replied.

"GET OUT RICHARD, GET OUT!"

Richard leaves the room and stands outside of his bedroom door up against the wall. Helen puts the babies to bed and goes to check on Richard. Mom, I have never seen Angela like this. "I know baby, I called Tina to check on her and Mr. Miller."

"Well, how are they?"

They are doing as well as expected, Mr. Miller is strong. Tina said he just keep saying it won't be long before he sees Grandma Peaches again. You know she lived to be 89, that is a blessing. I think you should call Pastor Brown. Ok, I will give him a call. Richard called pastor Brown and told him about Ashley and Angela's grieving condition. Pastor Brown drove himself to Atlanta leaving his wife and children home to offer the counselor Angela counsel. Pastor Brown was the only person Angela would talk to outside of Grandpa Miller. It took him a few days, but he soon had Angela laughing and eating again. Things were starting to get back to normal. After Pastor Brown, Left Angela with a word, they that wait on the Lord he will renew their strength, Isaiah 40:31." I sought the lord and he heard me and delivered me from all my fears Psalms 34:4."

Angela's greatest fear had come true she had lost her Grandma Peaches, but she knew God is her refuge and strength, a very present help in the time of trouble Psalms 46:1. She took things one day at a time, and slowly got back to her normal activities. Ashley and Spencer began to rebuild their marriage.

About a month later, Richard was called for an interview and was given the job. He explained to them from the onset that he was the pastor of a church, and he was only in search of a remote job, so he could run the church properly and he would report to the office once or twice a week. The employer agreed, it was as if God had set this particular Job for Richard because everything was going as planned. Things started to bounce back for Angela and Richard.

One fateful afternoon, Angela was in the office at church, she was attending to members who had come for counseling while the babysitter they had employed was looking after the children in the old children class that had then turned into a waiting room. Tina kept calling Angela while she was in the midst of counseling, Angela had to take the call and promised to call her back shortly. When the person had left, Angela quickly placed a call back to Tina. "Guess what?" she asked Angela.

"You know I'm bad at guessing." Angela replied to her, she never had the patience for guessing.

"He popped the question! I am getting married soon." She announced. "Thank you, Jesus! That is good news" Angela congratulated Tina. "You know what, this calls for a celebration. Once I am done with counseling, I will inform Richard about this, we need to celebrate." They said their goodbyes to each other and ended the call.

The next person who came in for counseling was Holly. "I just wanted to inform you that Cameron and I are expecting a child" she told Angela after they had exchanged pleasantries.

It was a good afternoon for Angela, good news was flying around. She congratulated Holly and prayed with her. This time, Angela was convinced in her spirit that this baby would make it and bring blessings to the life of the parents.